John Lyly's Campaspe: A Retelling

David Bruce

Published by David Bruce, 2022.

JOHN LYLY'S CAMPASPE: A RETELLING

First edition. October 25, 2022.

ISBN: 979-8215318287

Written by David Bruce.

Table of Contents

Cover Photograph for John Lyly's *Campaspe*: A Retelling
Jerzy Gorecki
https://pixabay.com/photos/woman-model-portrait-pose-style-6597788/

Educate Yourself
Read Like A Wolf Eats
Be Excellent to Each Other
Books Then, Books Now, Books Forever

In this retelling, as in all my retellings, I have tried to make the work of literature accessible to modern readers who may lack the knowledge about mythology, religion, and history that the literary work's contemporary audience had.

Do you know a language other than English? If you do, I give you permission to translate this book, copyright your translation, publish or self-publish it, and keep all the royalties for yourself. (Do give me credit, of course, for the original retelling.)

I would like to see my retellings of classic literature used in schools, so I give permission to the country of Finland (and all other countries) to give copies of this book to all students forever. I also give permission to the state of Texas (and all other states) to give copies of this book to all students forever. I also give permission to all teachers to give copies of this book to all students forever.

Teachers need not actually teach my retellings. Teachers are welcome to give students copies of my eBooks as background material. For example, if they are teaching Homer's *Iliad* and *Odyssey*, teachers are welcome to give students copies of my *Virgil's* Aeneid: *A Retelling in Prose* and tell students, "Here's another ancient epic you may want to read in your spare time."

CAST OF CHARACTERS

Alexander, King of Macedon. Conqueror of Greece. He is known in history as Alexander the Great.

Page to Alexander.

Melippus, Chamberlain to Alexander.

Hephestion, his General.

ALEXANDER'S WARRIORS:

Clitus, an officer.

Parmenio, an officer.

Milectus, a soldier.

Phrygius, a soldier.

PHILOSOPHERS AND THEIR SERVANTS:

Plato.

Granichus, Servant to Plato.

Aristotle.

Diogenes, Cynic philosopher.

Manes, Servant to Diogenes.

Chrysippus, Stoic philosopher.

Crates.

Cleanthes, Stoic philosopher.

Anaxarchus.

Apelles, a Painter.

Psyllus, Servant to Apelles.

Crysus, a beggar.

Solinus, a citizen of Athens.

Sylvius, a citizen of Athens.

Perim, Son to Sylvius.

Milo, Son to Sylvius.

Trico, Son to Sylvius.

Lais, a Courtesan, aka prostitute.

CAMPASPE, a female Theban Captive.

Timoclea, a female Theban Captive.

Citizens of Athens, other captive women, etc.

SCENE: Athens, Greece.

TIME: The story begins immediately after the Macedonians' defeat of Thebes in 335 B.C.E.

NOTES:

In this society, a person of higher rank would use "thou," "thee," "thine," and "thy" when referring to a person of lower rank. (These terms were also used affectionately and between equals.) A person of lower rank would use "you" and "your" when referring to a person of higher rank.

The word "wench" at this time was not necessarily negative. It was often used affectionately.

The word "fair" can mean attractive, beautiful, handsome, good-looking.

The *Oxford English Dictionary* defines "manners" as "A person's habitual behaviour or conduct; morals." This meaning is now obsolete.

In Lyly's play, the word "counterfeit" often means a painting.

In Lyly's play, the phrase "to shadow" often means "to paint."

"Sirrah" was a title used to address someone of a social rank inferior to the speaker. Friends, however, could use it to refer to each other, and fathers could call their sons "sirrah."

Oedipus, famous protagonist of a play by Sophocles, came from Thebes, as did his daughter Antigone, famous protagonist of another play by Sophocles.

Statius' *Thebaid* is an epic poem about Thebes. It tells of the conflict between the sons of Oedipus: Polynices and Eteocles.

Cynics believed that lives should be lived in accordance with virtue, which is the end of life. Virtue is much more important than pleasure.

Stoics pursued happiness based in virtue.

The Cynics and the Stoics both believed in virtuous conduct.

Diogenes of Sinope was a Cynic. He appears in Lyly's play.

The Cynics took as their symbol dogs, and so Diogenes is sometimes called Diogenes the Dog. The name "dog" is also a comment on the way he sometimes behaved toward others.

Cleanthes and Chrysippus were Stoics. They appear in Lyly's play.

Much later than the events of Lyly's play, in Roman times, Cicero, Seneca, and Roman Emperor Marcus Aurelius were Stoics.

John Lyly is writing drama, not history. Dramatists frequently take liberties with historical facts.

CHAPTER 1

— 1.1 —

Clitus and Parmenio, two generals in Alexander the Great's army, stood outside the walls of Athens, Greece. Alexander's Macedonian army had just defeated the city of Thebes in 335 B.C.E. Now Alexander ruled Greece.

Clitus said, "Parmenio, I cannot tell which quality I should more commend in Alexander's victories: courage or courtesy. In his courage he has a resolution without fear, and in his courtesy he has a liberality — a generosity — above custom.

"Thebes has been razed, and the people have not been tortured as if on a rack; towers have been thrown down, and bodies have not been thrust aside. This has been a conquest without conflict, and a cruel war in a mild peace."

Actually, in history Alexander had been harsh in his treatment of Thebes. His soldiers killed six thousand Thebans and sold the rest — thirty thousand Thebans — into slavery.

Alexander, however, treated the rest of the Greeks, including the Athenians, much better, and he was generous to individual Greeks at times.

Parmenio said:

"Clitus, it is fitting that the son of the late King Philip of Macedon is none other than Alexander. Seeing in the father a full perfection, who could have therefore doubted in the son an excellency?

"For as the moon can borrow nothing else of the sun but light, so of a sire, in whom nothing but virtue was, what else could the child receive other than excellence?

"It is for pieces of turquoise to stain each other, not for diamonds; in the one a difference in goodness can be made, in the other there is no comparison."

The colors of pieces of turquoise vary in brightness: Polished bright blue turquoise is especially prized. A highly prized piece of turquoise figuratively stains an inferior piece of turquoise next to it. Diamonds are transparent.

Clitus said, "You mistake me, Parmenio, if while I commend Alexander, you imagine I call Philip into question; unless perhaps you think (which no one of judgment will imagine) that because I like the fruit, therefore I heave at the tree; or coveting to kiss the child, I therefore go about to poison the teat."

"Heave" can mean "feel loathing" or "vomit."

"Aye, but Clitus, I perceive you are figuratively born in the east, and never laugh except at the sun rising," Parmenio said, "which is evidence that although you show a duty where you ought, yet you show no great devotion where you might."

Parmenio was punning on "sun." The sun rises, and Alexander, son of Philip, was rising.

"We will make no controversy of that which there ought to be no question," Clitus said. "Only this shall be the opinion of us both, that none was worthy to be the father of Alexander but Philip, nor was anyone worthy to be the son of Philip but Alexander."

"Quiet, Clitus, behold the spoils and prisoners! They are a pleasant sight to us, because profit is joined with honor; it is not much painful to the captive Thebans, because their captivity is eased by mercy."

Guarded, Timoclea, Campaspe, and other captives entered the scene. Some soldiers carried valuable spoils.

Timoclea said:

"Fortune, thou did never yet deceive virtue, because virtue never yet did trust fortune. Sword and fire will never get spoil where wisdom and fortitude bear sway."

Lady Fortune is a goddess who is represented as standing on a ball. One can easily fall off the ball, and in life, one can suffer bad luck. Lady Fortune also has a wheel that turns: the Wheel of Fortune. Those at the top of the wheel have a good and happy life, while those at the bottom of the wheel have a bad and unhappy life.

Timoclea continued:

"Oh, Thebes, thy walls were raised by the sweetness of the peaceful harp, but they were razed by the shrillness of the war trumpet."

According to mythology, twin brothers built the stone walls of Thebes. Zethus carried the stones, while Amphion played his lyre, a musical instrument, and stones rose in the air and floated to where they fit in the wall.

Timoclea continued:

"Alexander would never have come so near the walls, had Epaminondas walked about the walls, and the Thebans might still have been merry in their streets, if he had been alive to guard their towers."

Epaminondas was a Theban general in the years when the Thebans were fighting the Spartans.

Timoclea continued:

"But destiny is seldom foreseen, and it is never prevented.

"We are here now captives, whose necks are yoked by force, but whose hearts cannot yield by death.

"Come, Campaspe and the rest, and let us not be ashamed to cast our eyes on him, on whom we feared not to cast our arrows and spears."

The Theban captives were soon to see Alexander the Great.

"Madam, you need not fear," Parmenio said. "It is Alexander who is the conqueror."

He meant that Alexander was a merciful conqueror.

"Alexander has overcome, not conquered," Timoclea said.

"To bring all under his subjection is to conquer," Parmenio said.

"He cannot subdue that which is divine," Timoclea said.

"Thebes was not divine," Parmenio said.

"Virtue is divine," Timoclea said.

Clitus said:

"As Alexander cherishes virtue, so he will cherish you.

"He does not drink blood, but thirsts after honor; he is greedy for victory, but never satisfied with mercy. In fight he is terrifying, as befits a captain; in conquest he is mild, as befits a king."

"Never satisfied with mercy" is unclear. The parallelism of the sentence suggests that this is something nonviolent. Perhaps Alexander is not satisfied with one example of mercy and always wants more.

But "never satisfied with mercy" considered without parallelism suggests that Alexander prefers war to mercy.

Campaspe continued:

"In all things then, he is Alexander, than which nothing can be greater."

Campaspe said:

"Then if it be such a thing to be Alexander, I hope it shall be no miserable thing to be a virgin. For if he shall save our honors, it is more than to restore our goods. And I wish that he will preserve our reputations rather than our lives. If he does that, we will confess there can be no greater thing than to be Alexander."

Campaspe would soon become Alexander's concubine.

Alexander the Great, his general Hephestion, and some attendants entered the scene.

"Clitus, are these people prisoners?" Alexander the Great asked. "From where came these spoils?"

His army had conquered a large area, and Alexander could not be sure from where prisoners and spoils were coming to him.

"If it pleases your Majesty, they are prisoners, and they are from Thebes," Clitus answered.

"Of what calling or reputation are they?" Alexander the Great asked.

"I don't know, but they seem to be ladies of honor," Clitus said.

Alexander the Great said:

"I will find out."

He then said to Timoclea:

"Madam, from where you have come, I know; but who you are, I cannot tell."

Timoclea said, "Alexander, I am the sister of Theagines, who fought a battle with thy father before the city of Chyronie, where Theagines died valiantly. What I say about my brother's valor, none can contradict."

In 338 B.C.E. the battle of Chyronie (better known as Chaeronea) was fought in Boeotia.

Alexander the Great replied:

"Lady, there seem in your words valiant sparks of your brother's deeds, but worser fortune in your life than his death, but fear not, for you shall live without violence, enemies, or poverty."

He then asked Campaspe:

"But who are you, fair lady? Another sister to Theagines?"

"I am no sister to Theagines, but a humble handmaid to Alexander," Campaspe said. "I was born with a parentage neither the highest nor the lowest, and I was born to suffer extreme bad fortune."

Alexander the Great said:

"Well, ladies, for so your virtues show that you are ladies, whatsoever your births are, you shall be honorably treated. Athens shall be your Thebes, and you shall not be as abject subjects of war, but as subjects to Alexander."

He then ordered:

"Parmenio, conduct these honorable ladies into the city. Order the soldiers to not so much as in words to offer them any offence, and let all the ladies' needs be supplied, in so far forth as shall be necessary for such persons and my prisoners."

Parmenio and the Theban captives exited.

Alexander then said:

"Hephestion, it remains now that we have as great care to govern in peace, as we have had to conquer in war, so that while arms cease, arts may flourish, and joining letters with lances, we endeavor to be as good philosophers as soldiers, knowing it no less praise to be wise, than commendable to be valiant."

He had conquered Greece with weapons; now he wanted to rule Athens with peace.

Hephestion replied:

Your Majesty therein shows that you have as great desire to rule as to subdue.

"That commonwealth must necessarily be fortunate, whose captain is a philosopher, and whose philosopher is a captain."

Manes, Granichus, and Psyllus met on a street and talked. Manes and Granichus were servants to philosophers. Psyllus was a servant to a painter.

Manes was the servant to Diogenes the Cynic.

Granichus was the servant to Plato.

Psyllus was the servant to Apelles, a painter.

"Instead of a master, I serve a mouse, whose house is a tub, whose dinner is a crust, and whose bed is a board," Manes said.

Diogenes the Cynic once saw and admired a mouse that tended to its own business and did not chase luxuries. Diogenes sought to live a simple lifestyle. For a while, he lived in a tub.

"Then thou are in a state of life that philosophers commend. A crumb for thy supper, a hand for thy cup, and thy clothes for thy sheets," Psyllus said. "For *natura paucis contenta*."

After seeing a boy drinking water out of his cupped hand, Diogenes threw away his wooden bowl. Diogenes ate simple food, and he slept in his clothes.

The Latin means: "Nature is content with little."

Granichus said, "Manes, it is a pity that so proper — so handsome — a man should be cast away upon a philosopher, but that Diogenes that dog should have Manes that dogbolt, it grieves nature and spites art: the one [nature] having found thee so dissolute — I mean absolute — in body, and the other [art] so single — I mean singular — in mind."

Granichus was "accidentally" insulting Manes and then praising him. He insulted him by saying that he was dissolute in body and simple in mind. He praised him by saying that he was perfect (absolute) in body and preeminent (singular) in mind.

Diogenes was called the Dog, in part because of his rude manners, and in part because the Cynics adopted the dog as their symbol.

A dog-bolt is a menial servant.

"Are you merry?" Manes said. "It is a sign by the trip of your tongue, and the toys — the foolish trifles and fancies — of your head, that you have done something today that I have not done these three days."

Nature and art are different. Nature is a human's character, which can be changed by art — by the application of reason.

"What is that?" Psyllus asked.

"Dined," Manes answered.

"I think Diogenes keeps but cold cheer," Granichus said.

Diogenes' "cold cheer" is an austere lifestyle.

"I wish it were so, but he keeps neither hot nor cold," Manes said.

Cheer is also food and drink. Manes was saying that Diogenes lacked food, whether hot or cold.

"What then, lukewarm?" Granichus said. "That made Manes run from his master yesterday."

"Manes had reason to run away," Psyllus said, "for his name foretold as much."

"My name?" Manes said. "How so, sir boy?"

"You know that it is called *Mons, à movendo*, because it stands still," Psyllus said.

Some names are the opposite of what we would expect. For example, some obese men are nicknamed "Tiny."

From *movendum*, Latin for "moving," mountains get the name "mons," because they don't move. So said Psyllus.

"Good," Manes said.

"And thou are named *Manes, à manendo*, because thou run away," Psyllus said.

From *manendum*, Latin for "staying in place," Manes gets his name because he doesn't stay in place. So said Psyllus.

"Excellent reasoning!" Manes said. "I did not run away, but I did retire."

Like some soldiers, he did not run away, but instead made a strategic repositioning.

"To a prison, because thou would have leisure to contemplate," Psyllus said.

"I will prove that my body was immortal because it was in prison," Manes said.

"How?" Granichus asked.

"Didn't your masters ever teach you that the soul is immortal?" Manes asked.

"Yes," Granichus said.

"And the body is the prison of the soul," Manes said.

"True," Granichus said.

"Why then, thus to make my body immortal, I put it to prison," Manes said.

"Oh, bad!" Granichus said.

Bad reasoning, indeed.

"Excellent ill!" Psyllus said.

Excellent ill reasoning, indeed.

Manes said:

"You may see how dull a fasting wit is."

If he were fed better, he would be wittier and speak more intelligently.

"Therefore, Psyllus, let us go to supper with Granichus: Plato is the best fellow of all philosophers. Give me a master who reads a lecture in the morning in the school, and at noon in the kitchen."

Plato, famous for his *Dialogues*, kept the best table of the masters of these three servants. He was also easy-going.

"And so would I," Psyllus said.

"Ah, sirs, my master — Plato — is a king in his parlor for the body, and a god in his study for the soul," Granichus said. "When among all his men, he commends one who is an excellent musician, then I stand nearby, and clap another on the shoulder, and say, 'This is a surpassingly good cook.'"

Granichus valued food more than music.

"That is well done, Granichus," Manes said. "Give me pleasure that goes in at the mouth, not the ear. I had rather fill my guts than my brains."

Psyllus said:

"I serve Apelles, who feeds me as Diogenes does Manes, for at dinner the one preaches abstinence, and the other commends counterfeiting [painting].

"When I would eat meat, he paints a spit for roasting meat, and when I thirst, he asks, 'Isn't this a fair pot for holding an alcoholic beverage?' and points to a table in a painting that contains the banquet of the gods, where there are many dishes to feed the eye, but not to fill the gut."

"What do thou do then?" Granichus asked.

Psyllus said:

"This he then does: Bring in many examples that some have lived by savors [smells], and proves that it is much easier to grow fat by colors, and he tells about birds that have been fattened by painted grapes in winter, and how many have so fed their eyes with their mistress' picture that they never desired to take food, being glutted with the delight in their mistress' beauty.

"Then he shows me counterfeits [paintings], portraits of such people as have surfeited with their filthy and loathsome vomits, and have surfeited with the riotous bacchanales — the drunken orgies — of the god Bacchus and his disorderly crew, which are painted all to the life in his shop.

"To conclude, I fare hardly and with difficulty, though I go richly, which makes me when I should begin to shadow [portray] a lady's face, to draw a lamb's head, and sometimes to set to the body of a maid a shoulder of mutton: for *semper animus meus est in patinis*."

The Latin means: "Always my soul is in the stew pot."

In other words: I am always thinking about food.

Psyllus "goes richly": This may mean that he uses his imagination to picture food.

Manes said:

"Thou fare like a god in comparison to me: For if I could just see a cook's shop painted, I would make my eyes as fat as butter.

"For I have nothing but sentences to fill my maw, such as:

"*Plures occidit crapula quàm gladius.*"

The Latin means: "Overeating kills more than the sword."

Manes continued:

"*Musa ieiunantibus amica.*"

The Latin means: "The Muse is a friend to those who fast."

Manes continued:

"Repletion kills delicately.

"And an old saw of abstinence by Socrates:

"The belly is the head's grave.

"Thus with sayings, not with food, he makes a gallimaufry."

A gallimaufry is a stew.

"But how do thou then live?" Granichus asked.

"With fine jests, sweet air, and the dog's alms," Manes said.

The dog's alms are 1) scraps such as those thrown to a dog, or 2) gifts of food given to Diogenes the Dog.

"Well, for this time I will staunch thy hunger, and among pots and platters, thou shall see what it is to serve Plato," Granichus said.

"Out of joy for it, Granichus, let's sing," Psyllus said.

"My voice is as clear in the evening as in the morning," Manes said.

In other words: Fasting clears the voice.

Manes woke up hungry, and he was still hungry in the evening.

"That is another commodity — another advantage — of emptiness," Granichus said.

They began their song.

Granichus sang:

"O for a bowl of fat [rich] canary,

"Rich Palermo, sparkling sherry,

"Some nectar else, from Juno's dairy,

"O these draughts would make us merry."

Canary is sweet wine from the Canary Islands.

Palermo is wine from Palermo, Sicily.

Nectar is the drink of the gods.

Juno is the wife of Jove, aka Jupiter, king of the gods.

Psyllus sang:

"O for a wench. (I deal in faces,

"And in other daintier things.)

"Tickled am I with her embraces,

"Fine dancing in such fairy rings."

Fairy rings are literally circles in grass, and perhaps figuratively they are a circular part of a woman's anatomy.

"Things" can refer to genitalia.

"Dancing" probably means what you think it means, if you think prostitutes (and other women) give dance lessons.

Manes sang:

"O for a plump fat leg of mutton,

"Veal, lamb, capon [castrated rooster], pig, and cony [rabbit],

"None is happy but a glutton,

"None an ass, but who wants [lacks] money."

All sang the end of the song:

"Wines (indeed) and girls are good,

"But brave victuals feast the blood,

"For wenches, wine, and lusty cheer [robust food, or lusty entertainment],

"*Jove would leap down to surfeit here.*"
"To surfeit" means "to overindulge."

Melippus, Alexander's chamberlain, stood alone in a room of the palace.

He said to himself:

"I have never had such trouble to warn scholars to come before a king.

"First, I came to Chrysippus, a tall, lean, old, mad man, and I told him to appear immediately before Alexander. He stood staring at my face, moving neither his eyes nor his body. I urged him to give some answer, but he took up a book, sat down, and said nothing. Melissa, his maid, told me it was his manner, and that often she was obliged to thrust food into his mouth because he would rather starve than cease study.

"'Well,' I thought, 'seeing that bookish men are so blockish and obtuse, and seeing that great clerks are such simple-minded courtiers, I will be partaker neither of their commons — their community meals — nor of their commendations.'

"From thence I came to Plato and to Aristotle, and to various others, with none refusing to come, except an old obscure fellow, who sitting in a tub turned towards the sun, read Greek to a young boy.

"When I told him to appear before Alexander, he answered, 'If Alexander would like to see me, let him come to me; if he would like to learn about and from me, let him come to me; whatsoever he wants, let him come to me.'

"'Why,' I said, 'he is a king.'

"He answered, 'Why, I am a philosopher.'

"I said, 'Why, but he is Alexander.'

"He answered, 'Aye, but I am Diogenes.'

"I was half angry to see one so crooked in his shape being so crabby and disagreeable in his utterances. So going my way, I said, 'Thou shall repent it, if thou do not come to Alexander.'

"'Nay,' he, smiling, answered. 'Alexander may repent it, if he does not come to Diogenes: Virtue must be sought, not offered.'"

Diogenes' teacher, Antisthenes, was reluctant to accept Diogenes as a student, but Diogenes was patient and waited to be accepted. Laertius, in his *Lives of Eminent Philosophers*, wrote, "On reaching Athens [Diogenes] fell in with Antisthenes. Being repulsed by him, because he never welcomed students, by sheer persistence Diogenes wore him out."

Antisthenes even beat Diogenes with a stick in an attempt to drive him away. Such tests are common in Taoism and Zen Buddhism. Teachers will say "no" at first and wait for the would-be student to go away. If the would-be student stays and waits for days, the teacher knows that the student is sincere about acquiring knowledge. Some Zen masters have even poured the contents of slop buckets on would-be students' heads to test their determination.

Wandering warrior Zhang Liang once met an old man on a bridge. The old man deliberately kicked off a sandal, then asked Zhang Liang to retrieve it and to put it back on his foot. After Zhang Liang had done so, the old man told him that he was worthy to be taught and to meet him at the bridge in the early morning in five days. Five days later, Zhang Liang arrived at the bridge a few minutes after daybreak, and the old man told him to arrive earlier in another five days. Five days later, Zhang Liang arrived at the bridge earlier, but the old man was already there and told him, "Arrive earlier in another five days' time. This is your last chance." Five days later, Zhang Liang arrived at the bridge around midnight, and the old man arrived a few minutes later. The old man, who was named Huang Shi Gong, then taught Zhang Liang the military strategy that enabled him to help Liu Bang become the founder of the Han Dynasty.

Melippus concluded:

"And so turning himself to his cell, he grunted I don't know what, like a pig under a tub.

"But I must be gone because the philosophers are coming."

He exited.

The philosophers Plato, Aristotle, Cleanthes, Anaxarchus, Crates, and Chrysippus entered the scene.

John Lyly did not write history. Plato was dead at this time, but Aristotle, Anaxarchus, and Crates were alive. Cleanthes and Chrysippus were not yet born in 335 B.C.E.

Oddly, all these ancient Greek philosophers knew Latin well.

John Lyly is also not writing clear philosophy. In this scene, Plato will argue for a supernatural explanation of events in nature, and Aristotle sometimes will seem to be arguing for a natural explanation of events in nature and sometimes will seem to believe in a god.

In reading the argument below, note that Plato and Aristotle both believed in a Prime Mover, aka Unmoved Mover.

When it comes to understanding difficult concepts, defining important terms is a big help. Often, people have very different definitions of God.

The *Oxford English Dictionary* defines "prime mover" as "A person who instigates or originates something; spec. God regarded as the motive force of the universe."

Plato said, "It is a difficult controversy, Aristotle, and rather to be wondered at than believed, how natural causes should work supernatural effects."

Natural causes come from nature, without any help from anything supernatural.

God is supernatural. Morality and reason also seem to be supernatural.

The controversy the philosophers were discussing was whether God existed and caused natural events to happen.

Aristotle said, "I do not so much maintain the view that the apparition that is seen in the moon, nor the *demonium* of Socrates, as that I cannot by natural reason give any reason for the ebbing and flowing of the sea, which makes me in the depth of my studies cry out, '*O ens entium, miserere mei.*'"

The Latin means: "Oh, essence of essences, take pity on me."

"Apparition" refers to the visibility of a heavenly, aka astronomical, body. The moon moves, and the reason why it moves is not visible.

The *Oxford English* Dictionary defines the astronomical meaning of "apparition" in this way: "The state or condition of being manifest to sight, or of being visible; *esp.* the visibility of a star, planet, or comet."

Today, we know that the tides of the sea have a natural cause: They are caused by the gravitational pull of the moon.

Socrates' *demonium* was his conscience, which gave him guidance.

Does anything supernatural exist? If reality consists of *only* matter, space, and energy, then how can ethics and morality (and logic and reason) exist?

C.S. Lewis (1898-1963) made an argument from morality for the existence of God. See "NOTES," located before the appendixes.

Aristotle's Latin sentence can be understood to reflect belief in one god, rather than the many gods of paganism.

Here, as in history, Aristotle is a seeker after truth. Here, he is asking whether God exists and causes such natural phenomena as the tides.

Plato said to Aristotle:

"Cleanthes and you attribute so much to nature by searching for things that are not to be found, that while you study a cause [a particular case] of your own, you omit the occasion [reason why things are as they are] itself.

"There is no man so savage in whom this divine particle does not rest: that there is an omnipotent, eternal, and divine mover, which may be called God."

According to Plato, the philosophers Aristotle and Cleanthes investigate individual cases of natural phenomena that need explaining, but they don't look at the big picture: Why do things exist and why do they change? Plato believes in a Prime Mover, which is God.

The Prime Mover is not caused, but it causes everything else. The Prime Mover has necessary existence.

We may think of the Prime Mover as causing the existence of the universe and keeping it in existence each moment.

In the history of philosophy, Aristotle believed in God as an Unmoved Mover. God causes change, but God is unchanged.

Saint Thomas Aquinas made five arguments for the existence of God, including arguments for the existence of a Unmoved Mover or Prime Mover, which he says we call God. See "NOTES," located before the appendixes.

Cleanthes said:

"I am of this mind, that the First Mover, which you term God, is the instrument of all the movings that we attribute to nature. The earth, which is mass, swims on the sea; seasons divided in themselves, fruits growing in themselves, the majesty of the sky, the whole firmament of the world, and whatsoever else appears to be miraculous, what man almost of mean capacity but can prove it natural?"

This seems to be confused: Cleanthes' first sentence states that all of these natural events can be explained by the First Mover, whom philosophers call God.

But the end of the paragraph states that all of these natural events can be explained by natural causes without having recourse to a supernatural being, and even a man of limited intelligence can prove it.

Perhaps Cleanthes regards the First Mover as Nature and not as God?

Come on, philosophers, define your terms so the rest of us can figure out what you mean!

Anaxarchus said, "These causes shall be debated at our philosophers' feast, in which controversy I will take part with Aristotle, that there is *Natura naturans*, and yet not God."

Natura naturans is a Latin phrase that means "nature doing nature" or "nature does what nature does."

Plato's belief in a Prime Mover, which Aristotle called an Unmoved Mover, and Cleanthes called the First Mover, is consistent with belief in a Judeo-Christian god, but belief in a Judeo-Christian god requires much more than belief in a Prime Mover.

"And I will argue with Plato that there is *Deus optimus maximus*, and not nature," Crates said.

The Latin *Deus optimus maximus* means "God the best and greatest."

"Here comes Alexander," Aristotle said.

Alexander the Great, Hephestion, Parmenio, and Clitus entered the scene. Cleanthes was Alexander's general, and Parmenio and Clitus were officers in Alexander's army.

"I see, Hephestion, that these philosophers are here waiting for us," Alexander the Great said.

"They would not be philosophers, if they did not know their duties," Hephestion said.

"But I much marvel that Diogenes should be so dogged — so perverse and spiteful," Alexander the Great said.

"I can't help but think that his excuse will be better than Melippus' message," Hephestion said.

In other words: Hephestion expected that Diogenes would be much more polite when he saw Alexander in person.

Alexander the Great said:

"I will go see him, Hephestion, because I long to see the man who would command Alexander to come."

He then addressed the philosophers:

"Aristotle and the rest, since my coming from Thebes to Athens, from a place of conquest to a palace of quiet, I have resolved with myself to have as many philosophers in my court, as I had soldiers in my camp.

"My court shall be a school wherein I wish to see practiced as great doctrine in peace, as I did discipline in war."

Aristotle replied, "We are all here ready to be commanded, and glad we are that we are commanded because nothing better becomes kings than literature and book learning, which makes them come as near to the gods in wisdom as they do in dignity."

Alexander the Great said, "That is true, Aristotle, but yet there is among you, yes, and one of your bringing up, one who sought to destroy Alexander. His name is Callistenes, Aristotle, and the reasons of his philosophy shall not make allowances for his treasons against his prince."

Callistenes was Aristotle's student and the son of Hero, his niece.

"If ever mischief entered into the heart of Callistenes, let Callistenes suffer for it, but Aristotle denies that Aristotle ever imagined any such thing of Callistenes," Aristotle replied.

Alexander the Great said:

"Well, Aristotle, his being your relative may blind thee, and that I am personally involved may blind me, but in kings' causes I will not listen to and abide by scholars' arguments.

"The purpose of this meeting shall be for a commandment that you all frequent my court, instruct the young with rules, confirm the old with reasons. Let your lives be answerable to your learnings, lest my proceedings be contrary to my promises."

"You said you would ask every one of them a question, which yesterday evening none of us could answer," Hephestion said.

Alexander the Great said:

"I will.

"Plato, of all beasts, which is the subtlest and craftiest?"

"That which man hitherto never knew," Plato answered.

Apparently, subtle and crafty animals stay out of the sight of man.

Alexander the Great asked, "Aristotle, how should a man be thought to be a god?"

"By doing a thing impossible for a man," Aristotle answered.

Dying and then rising three days later would be sufficient.

Alexander the Great asked, "Chrysippus, which was first, the day or the night?"

"The day, by a day," Chrysippus answered.

A 24-hour day includes day and night. Night is on average 12 hours.

Alexander the Great said:

"Indeed! Strange questions must have strange answers.

"Cleanthes, what do you say: Is life or death the stronger?"

"Life, which suffers so many troubles," Cleanthes answered.

Dead people don't have to worry about such things as taxes.

Alexander the Great asked, "Crates, how long should a man live?"

"Until he thinks it is better to die than to live," Crates answered.

Alexander the Great asked, "Anaxarchus, which brings forth the most creatures: the sea or the earth?"

"The earth, for the sea is just a part of the earth," Anaxarchus answered.

Alexander the Great said, "Hephestion, I think they have answered all the questions well, and I mean often to test them in such questions."

Hephestion replied, "It is better to have in your court a wise man, than in your ground a golden mine. Therefore, I would leave war and instead study wisdom if I were Alexander."

Alexander the Great said:

"So would I — if I were Hephestion.

"But come, let us go and grant the freedom that I promised to our Theban slaves."

Alexander the Great, Hephestion, Parmenio, and Clitus exited.

The philosophers began to walk to the marketplace.

"Thou are fortunate, Aristotle, that Alexander is thy scholar," Plato said.

This is true in history: Aristotle did tutor Alexander the Great.

"And all of you are happy and fortunate that he is your sovereign," Aristotle said.

"I could like the man well, if he could be contented to be just a man," Chrysippus said.

"He seeks to draw near to the gods in knowledge, not to be a god," Aristotle said.

Having arrived at the marketplace, the philosophers saw Diogenes the Cynic in his tub.

Plato said:

"Let us talk a little with Diogenes and ask why he didn't go with us to Alexander."

He then said:

"Diogenes, thou did forget thy duty, in that thou did not go with us to the king."

From his tub, Diogenes said, "And you did forget your profession as philosophers, in that you went to the king. "

According to Diogenes, seekers after truth — philosophers — rank higher than kings.

"Thou take as great pride in being peevish, as others glory in being virtuous," Plato said.

"And thou take as great honor in being a philosopher to be thought court-like, as others who are courtiers shame to be accounted philosophers," Diogenes said.

Diogenes believed that philosophers ought not to subordinate themselves to kings.

"These austere manners set aside, it is well known that thou did counterfeit money," Aristotle said.

In history, either Diogenes or his father adulterated currency. Diogenes then left his town of Sinope and went into exile.

Diogenes replied, "And it is well known that thou counterfeited thy manners, in that thou did not counterfeit money."

Hmm. Interesting insult. By not counterfeiting money, Aristotle is hiding his true nature, which is such that he would counterfeit money.

The *Oxford English Dictionary* defines "manners" as "A person's habitual behaviour or conduct; morals." This meaning is now obsolete.

"Thou have reason to contemn and scorn the court, being both in body and mind too crooked for a courtier," Aristotle said.

"It is as good to be crooked, and endeavor to make myself straight away from the court, as it is to be straight, and learn to be crooked at the court," Diogenes replied.

"Crooked" can mean "corrupt," and "straight" can mean "honest."

Crates said, "Thou think it a grace to be opposite against Alexander."

"And thou to be jump with — to be in sync with — and be in agreement with Alexander," Diogenes said.

"Let us go," Anaxarchus said, "for in contemning and scorning him, we shall better please him, than in staring and marveling at him."

"Plato, what do thou think of Diogenes?" Aristotle asked.

Plato said:

"To be Socrates, furious. Let us go."

According to Laertius Diogenes, author of *Lives of Eminent Philosophers*, Plato once referred to Diogenes as "Socrates gone mad."

CHAPTER 2

— 2.1 —

Holding a lantern, Diogenes walked down one side of a street.

Psyllus, Manes, and Granichus walked down the other side.

Psyllus said, "Behold, Manes, where thy master is; he is seeking either bones for his dinner, or pins to hold together his clothing. I will go and greet him."

"Do so," Manes said. "But be mum. Don't say a word about you seeing Manes."

"Then stay thou behind, and I will go with Psyllus," Granichus said.

Granichus and Psyllus walked over to Diogenes.

"All hail Diogenes to your proper person," Psyllus said.

"To your proper person" means "to you."

"All hate to thy peevish conditions," Diogenes said.

"O dog!" Granichus said.

"What do thou seek for here?" Psyllus asked.

"For a man and a beast," Diogenes answered.

Some retellings of this anecdote state that Diogenes said that he was looking for an *honest* man.

"That is easy to be found without thy light," Granichus said. "Aren't all these men?"

"They are called men, but they are not necessarily men," Diogenes said.

"What beast is it thou look for?" Granichus asked.

"The beast is my serving-man, Manes," Diogenes answered.

"He is a beast indeed if he will serve thee," Psyllus said.

"So is he who begat thee," Diogenes replied.

"What would thou do if thou were to find Manes?" Granichus asked.

"Give him permission to do as he had done before," Diogenes replied.

"What's that?" Granichus asked.

"To run away," Diogenes replied.

"Why, have thou no need of Manes?" Psyllus asked.

"It would be a shame for Diogenes to have need of Manes, and it would be a shame for Manes to have no need of Diogenes," Diogenes said.

"But assume that he were gone, would thou hire and take into service any of us two?" Granichus asked.

"Upon condition," Diogenes said.

"What condition?" Psyllus asked.

"That you tell me why and to what end any of you two were good," Diogenes said.

"Why, I am a scholar, and well skilled in philosophy," Granichus said.

"And I am an apprentice, and well skilled in painting," Psyllus said.

Diogenes said:

"Well, then, Granichus, be thou a painter to amend thine ill face.

"And be thou, Psyllus, a philosopher to correct thine evil way of life."

Catching sight of a man, Diogenes said:

"But who is that?

"Manes?"

"I don't care who I am, as long as I am not Manes," Manes said.

Granichus said to Manes, "You are taken tardy: You have been caught unawares."

"Let us slip aside, Granichus, to see the salutation between Manes and his master," Psyllus said.

Granichus and Psyllus stepped aside and eavesdropped.

Diogenes said:

"Manes, thou know that yesterday I threw away my dish, to drink in my hand, because my dish was superfluous.

"Now I am determined to put away my serving-man, and serve myself: *Quia non egeo tui vel te.*"

The Latin means: "Because I do not need you or what is yours."

Manes replied, "Master, you know a while ago I ran away, and so I mean to do again: *quia scio tibi non esse argentum.*"

The Latin means: "Because I know that you have no silver [no money]."

"I know I have no money, neither will I ever have a serving-man, for I was resolved long since to put away both my slaves: money and Manes," Diogenes said.

"So was I determined to shake off both my dogs: hunger and Diogenes," Manes said.

Hunger is a dog because in Greek and Latin, hunger barks.

Hunger and Diogenes are both dogging Manes.

"O sweet concent — musical concord — between a crowd and a Jew's harp," Psyllus said.

One meaning of "a crowd" is a fiddle.

A Jew's harp is also known as a jaw harp.

"Come, let us reconcile them," Granichus said.

"There is no need, for this is their customary behavior," Psyllus said. "Now they dine one upon another."

Diogenes exited.

"How are things now, Manes?" Granichus asked. "Have thou left thy master?"

"No, I did but just now bind myself to him," Manes said.

In other words: Arguing brought them closer together.

"Why, you were at mortal jars — deadly quarrels," Psyllus said.

"Indeed, no," Manes said. "We broke a bitter jest one upon the other."

"Why, thou are as dogged as he," Granichus said.

"My father knew them both when they were little whelps," Psyllus said.

Whelps are 1) puppies, or 2) impertinent young boys.

"Well, I will hurry after my master," Manes said.

"Why, is it supper time with Diogenes?" Granichus asked.

"Aye, with him at all times when he has food," Manes said.

Whenever Diogenes has food, it is time to eat.

"Why then, let every man go to his home, and let us steal out again and meet soon," Psyllus said.

"Where shall we meet?" Granichus asked.

"Why, at *Alae vendibili suspense hedera non est Opus*," Psyllus said.

The Latin means: "There is no need for a sign of ivy where the ale is good."

They would meet at the regular place: a place with good ale.

Ivy was often found outside inns. It served as a kind of sign.

"O Psyllus, *habeo te loco parentis*," Manes said. "Thou bless me."

The Latin means: "I consider you to be my parent."

Parents blessed their children.

They exited.

— 2.2 —

Alexander the Great, Hephestion, and a page stood in a room inside the palace.

Alexander the Great said to the page:

"Stand aside, sir boy, until you are called."

He then asked:

"Hephestion, how do you like the sweet face of Campaspe?"

"I cannot but commend the stout and undaunted courage of Timoclea," Hephestion said.

"Without doubt Campaspe had some great man as her father," Alexander the Great said.

"You know Timoclea had Theagines as her brother," Hephestion said.

"The name of Timoclea is still in thy mouth! Aren't thou in love?" Alexander the Great said.

"Not I," Hephestion said.

Alexander the Great said:

"Not with Timoclea, you mean; in this, you resemble the lapwing, who cries most where her nest is not."

Lapwings would pretend to have a wounded wing when predators would get close to their nest. A lapwing would cry and draw the predator away from the nest, and then the lapwing would take flight.

Alexander the Great continued:

"And so in order to lead me away from spying your love for Campaspe, you cry 'Timoclea.'"

Hephestion replied, "If I could subdue kingdoms as well as I can my thoughts, or if I were as far from ambition as I am from love, then all the world would account me as valiant in arms as I know that I myself am moderate in affection and love."

Hephestion had great skill in controlling thoughts of love, and he wished that he had as great skill in conquering nations.

"Is love a vice?" Alexander the Great asked.

"It is no virtue," Hephestion answered.

Alexander the Great said:

"Well, now thou shall see what small difference I make between Alexander and Hephestion.

"And since thou have been always partaker of my triumphs, thou shall be partaker of my torments.

"I am in love, Hephestion! I am in love! I love Campaspe, a thing far unfit for a Macedonian, for a king, for Alexander.

"Why do thou hang down thy head, Hephestion? Are thou blushing to hear that which I am not ashamed to tell?"

"If my words might crave pardon, and my counsel might crave credit, I would both discharge the duty of a subject, for so I am, and the office of a friend, for so I will," Hephestion said.

He had things to tell Alexander that Alexander would not like to hear.

"Speak, Hephestion," Alexander the Great said, "for whatsoever is spoken, Hephestion speaks to Alexander."

The two men respected each other.

Hephestion said:

"I cannot tell, Alexander, whether the report is more shameful to be heard, or the cause is more sorrowful to be believed?

"What! Has the son of Philip, King of Macedon, become the subject of Campaspe, the captive of Thebes?

"Has that mind, whose greatness the world could not contain, been drawn within the compass of a trifling, alluring eye?

"Will you handle the spindle with Hercules, when you should shake the spear with Achilles?"

Hercules once worked for three years for Omphale, the Queen of Lydia. She often wore his lionskin while he wore women's clothing and worked at a loom and spun thread and wound it onto a spindle.

Hephestion continued:

"Has the warlike sound of the military drum and trumpet been turned to the soft noise of lyre and lute?

"Have the neighing of barbed — armed — steeds, whose loudness filled the air with terror, and whose breaths dimmed the sun with vapor, been converted into delicate tunes and amorous glances?

"O Alexander, that soft and yielding mind should not be in him, whose hard and unconquered heart has made so many yield and surrender.

"But you love — ah, grief! But whom do you love?

"Campaspe? Ah, shame!

"She is a maiden truly unknown, she is unnoble, and who can tell whether she is immodest and wanton?

"She is a maiden whose eyes are framed by art to enamor, and whose heart was made by nature to enchant.

"Aye, but she is beautiful; yes, but she is not therefore chaste.

"Aye, but she is comely in all parts of the body, but she may be crooked in some part of the mind.

"Aye, but she is wise; yes, but she is a woman!

"Beauty is like the blackberry, which seems red when it is not ripe, resembling precious stones that are polished with honey, which the smoother they look, the sooner they break.

"It is thought wonderful among the seamen that mugil [grey mullet], which is of all fishes the swiftest, is found in the belly of the bret [turbot], which is of all fishes the slowest.

"And shall it not seem monstrous to wise men that the heart of the greatest conqueror of the world should be found in the hands of the weakest creature of nature? Of a woman? Of a captive?

"Ermines have fair skins, but foul livers; sepulchers have fresh colors, but rotten bones; women have fair faces, but false hearts."

Sepulchers, aka tombs, can have beautiful colors, but no matter how beautifully colored they are, they have rotten bones inside.

Hephestion continued:

"Remember, Alexander, thou have a camp to govern, not a bed-chamber.

"Don't fall from the armor of Mars to the arms of Venus.

"Don't go from the fiery assaults of war to the maidenly skirmishes of love.

'Don't go from displaying the eagle in thine ensign — thine battle flag — to set down the sparrow."

Sparrows, reputed to be lusty, were called the birds of Venus.

Hephestion continued:

"I sigh, Alexander, that where fortune could not conquer, folly should overcome.

"But behold all the perfection that may be in Campaspe; a hair curling by nature, not art; sweet alluring eyes; a fair face made to spite and in spite of

Venus, and a stately bearing in disdain of Juno, Queen of the gods; a wit and intelligence apt to understand, and quick to answer; a skin as soft as silk, and as smooth as jet; a long white hand, a fine little foot.

"To conclude, she has all parts answerable to the best part — but so what?

"Although she has heavenly gifts, virtue and beauty, isn't she made of earthly metal and substance, flesh and blood?

"You, Alexander, who would be a god, show yourself in this worse than a man, so soon to be both overseen and overtaken — that is, deceived — in a woman, whose false tears know their true and best times to flow, whose smooth and flattering words wound deeper than sharp swords.

"There is no surfeit — no over-indulging — as dangerous as over-indulging in honey, nor is there any poison as deadly as that of love; in the one medicine cannot prevail, and in the other counsel cannot prevail."

A proverb stated, "Words hurt more than swords."

Alexander the Great replied:

"My case would be light and trifling, Hephestion, and not worthy to be called love, if reason were a remedy, or if wise sentences and proverbs could salve and heal that which sense and perception cannot understand.

"Little do you know, and therefore slightly and slightingly do you regard, the dead embers in a private person, or live coals in a great prince, whose passions and thoughts do as far exceed others in the most extreme degree, as their callings do in majesty. An eclipse in the sun is more than the falling of a star; none can conceive the torments of a king, unless he is a king, whose desires are not inferior to their dignities: their high office and worthiness.

"And then judge, Hephestion, if the agonies of love are dangerous in a subject, whether they are not more than deadly to Alexander, whose deep and not-to-be-imagined sighs cleave and split the heart in pieces; and whose wounded thoughts can be neither expressed nor endured.

"Cease then, Hephestion, with arguments to seek to repulse love, which with their deity and godlike might, the gods cannot resist; and let this suffice to answer thee, that it is a king who loves, and it is Alexander who loves, whose affections are not to be measured by reason, being immortal, nor, I fear, are to be borne, being intolerable."

Alexander had pretensions of being a god. He was influenced by foreign ideas, and when he was in Egypt, he was called the son of Jupiter. Possibly, however, he was calling his affections and love immortal.

"I must necessarily yield, when neither reason nor counsel can be heard," Hephestion said.

"Yield, Hephestion, for Alexander does love, and therefore Alexander must obtain his love," Alexander the Great said.

Hephestion said:

"Suppose she doesn't love you.

"Affection and love do not come into existence by appointment or birth.

"Love that is forced is hated."

"I am a king, and I will command," Alexander the Great said.

"You may force someone to yield to your lust," Hephestion said, "but you cannot use fear to force someone to consent to love you."

A proverb stated, "Love cannot be compelled."

"Why, what is that which Alexander may not conquer as he wishes?" Alexander the Great asked.

"Why, that which you say the gods cannot resist: love," Hephestion answered.

Alexander the Great said:

"I am a conqueror, and she is a captive. I am as fortunate as she is fair. My greatness may grant her what she needs, and the gifts of my mind may raise the modest capability of her mind.

"Isn't it likely then that she should love? Isn't it reasonable?"

"You say that in love there is no reason, and therefore there can be no likelihood," Hephestion said.

Alexander the Great said:

"Let's discuss this no more, Hephestion. In this case I will use my own counsel, and in all other cases I will use thine advice. Thou may be a good soldier, but thou shall never be a good lover.

"Call my page."

The page stepped forward.

Alexander the Great ordered:

"Sirrah, go immediately to Apelles, and tell him to come to me without either delay or excuse."

"I go," the page said.

He exited.

Alexander the Great said:

"In the meantime, to recreate my spirits, being so near, we will go and see Diogenes.

"And look, we can see where his tub is."

He called:

"Diogenes!"

"Who calls?" Diogenes asked.

Alexander the Great replied:

"It is Alexander."

He then asked:

"How did it happen that you would not come out of your tub and go to my palace?"

"Because it was as far from my tub to your palace, as from your palace to my tub," Diogenes said.

"Why, then, do thou owe no reverence to kings?" Alexander the Great asked.

"No," Diogenes said.

"Why so?" Alexander the Great asked.

"Because they are no gods," Diogenes said.

"They are gods of the earth," Alexander the Great said.

"Yes, gods of earth," Diogenes said.

In other words: Kings are gods made of earth: flesh and blood.

"Plato is not of thy mind," Alexander the Great said.

"I am glad of it," Diogenes said.

"Why?" Alexander the Great asked.

"Because I would have no one have Diogenes' mind, except Diogenes," Diogenes said.

"If Alexander has anything that may pleasure Diogenes, let me know, and take it," Alexander the Great said.

"Then don't take from me that which you cannot give me, the light of the world," Diogenes said.

According to Laertius, when Alexander offered Diogenes anything he wanted, Diogenes, who was in Alexander's shadow, said, "Stand out of my light."

"What do thou want?" Alexander the Great asked.

"Nothing that you have," Diogenes said.

"I have the world at command," Alexander the Great said.

"And I hold the world in contempt," Diogenes said.

"Thou shall live no longer than I will allow you to live," Alexander the Great said.

"But I shall die whether or not you will my death," Diogenes said.

"How should one learn to be content?" Alexander the Great asked.

"Unlearn to covet," Diogenes said.

Alexander the Great said, "Hephestion, if I were not Alexander, I would wish to be Diogenes."

According to Plutarch in his "Life of Alexander," after hearing Alexander's words, Diogenes said, "If I were not Diogenes, I would wish to be Diogenes."

Hephestion said, "He is dogged and spiteful, but he is discreet and wise. I cannot tell how sharp he is, but he has a kind of sweetness. He is full of wit, yet he is too, too wayward and perverse."

"Diogenes, when I come this way again, I will both see thee and confer with thee," Alexander the Great said.

"Do," Diogenes said.

Alexander the Great said:

"But here comes Apelles."

Alexander's page returned, bringing Apelles the painter with him.

Alexander the Great asked:

"How are things now, Apelles? Is your painting of Venus' face finished yet?"

Venus is the goddess of sexual passion; her Greek name is Aphrodite.

"Not yet," Apelles said. "Beauty is not so soon shadowed [painted] and depicted because its perfection does not come within the compass either of cunning and skill or of color."

Alexander the Great said, "Well, let it rest unperfect and incomplete, and come with me, where I will show you beauty that is finished by nature, beauty that you have been trifling about by art."

Campaspe had been finished by nature: She was perfect.

Apelles' painting of Venus had not been finished: It was imperfect.
They exited.

CHAPTER 3

— 3.1 —

Apelles, Campaspe, and Psyllus talked together in a room in Apelles' house.

Apelles said, "Lady, I doubt whether there is any color so fresh and bright that may shadow [paint] a countenance as fair as yours."

Campaspe modestly replied, "Sir, I had thought you had been commanded to paint with your hand, not to gloss and flatter with your tongue; but as I have heard, it is the hardest thing in painting to set down a hard face, which makes you despair of painting my face; and then you shall have as great thanks to spare your labor, as you would have discredit to your art and skill if you persisted."

In other words: I am ugly, and painting an ugly face is difficult. If you attempt to paint my face, you will get a bad reputation as an artist, so it best for you not to paint me.

Campaspe was beautiful, and her saying that she has a hard face — an ugly face — was modesty.

Apelles said:

"Mistress, you neither differ from yourself nor your sex: for knowing your own perfection, you seem to dispraise that which men most commend, drawing and attracting them by that means into an admiration, where feeding themselves they fall into an ecstasy.

"Your modesty causes men's admiration of you, and your affections cause men to be sent into an ecstasy."

In other words: Campaspe was beautiful, and Apelles believed she knew it, but she, like other women, disparaged her beauty. But her beauty caused men to admire her; she was also modest, and that and the other qualities of her character caused men to pursue her and fall into an ecstasy of love.

Campaspe replied, "I am too young to understand your speech, although I am old enough to withstand your trap: You have been so long used to colors, you can do nothing but color."

She was punning: "Color" means "dissemble": to hide one's real intentions, motives, and feelings.

Apelles said:

"Indeed, I fear that the colors I see will alter the color I have."

He may blush.

Apelles continued:

"But come, madam, will you draw near, for Alexander will be here soon.

"Psyllus, stay here at the window, and if anyone enquires for me, answer, *Non lubet esse domi.*"

The Latin means: "He doesn't like to be at home."

They exited into Apelles' art studio.

Psyllus stood outside Apelles' art studio.

He said to himself:

"It is always my master's fashion, when any beautiful gentlewoman is to be drawn within, to make me stay outside."

Apelles liked to be alone with beautiful women.

Psyllus continued:

"But if he should paint Jupiter like a bull, like a swan, or like an eagle, then Psyllus with one hand must grind colors, and with the other he must hold the candle so Apelles can see to paint."

Apelles often painted mythological themes.

The gods are shape-shifters, and Jupiter used this ability to have affairs with mortal women:

1) Disguised as a bull, Jupiter kidnapped the Phoenician woman Europa, who climbed on his back. He then swam to Crete, where Europa bore him a son: King Midas.

2) Disguised as a swan, Jupiter seduced Leda, who bore him two daughters: Helen, who later became known as Helen of Troy, and Clytemnestra, who married and later murdered Agamemnon, leader of the Greek forces against the Trojans.

3) Disguised as an eagle, Jupiter kidnapped the beautiful boy Ganymede, who became his cupbearer, and, some say, his catamite. A catamite is a boy kept to serve as a sexual object for a homosexual man.

Psyllus continued:

"But let Apelles alone; the better he shadows her face, the more will he burn his own heart.

"Shadows" can mean 1) paints, and 2) protects from the sun.

Psyllus continued:

"And now if any man could meet with Manes, who, I dare say, looks as lean as if Diogenes dropped out of his nose —"

A proverb states: Hunger dropped out of his nose.

Manes entered the scene, just in time to hear Psyllus' last few words.

Manes said, "And here comes Manes, who has as much meat in his stomach as thou have honesty in thy head."

"Then I hope thou are very hungry," Psyllus said.

He was joking. If Manes had a stomach empty of food, then Psyllus would have a head empty of honesty.

"They who know thee, know that you are the type of person to wish me to be hungry — and know that you have a head empty of honesty," Manes said.

"But don't thou remember that we have certain liquor to confer with?" Psyllus asked.

They were supposed to meet at a tavern.

"Aye, but I have business," Manes said. "I must go cry a thing."

"Cry a thing" means "make a proclamation" — for example, about lost and found items.

"Why, what have thou lost?" Psyllus asked.

"That which I never had: my dinner," Manes said.

"Foul lubber, will thou cry for thy dinner?" Psyllus asked.

A "lubber" is a dolt.

Psyllus was using "cry" in the sense of "weep."

"I mean, I must cry," Manes said. "I must cry not as one would say 'cry,' but 'cry' — that is make a noise."

"Why, fool, that is all one," Psyllus said, "for if thou cry, thou must necessarily make a noise."

Manes said:

"Boy, thou are deceived. The word 'cry' has diverse meanings, and the word 'cry' may be assigned and applied to many things.

"The word 'knave' has only one meaning, and it can be applied only to thee."

"Profound Manes!" Psyllus said.

Manes had won the battle of puns.

"We Cynics are mad fellows," Manes said. "Didn't thou find I did quip thee?"

Manes was a Cynic, like his master: Diogenes. Like his master, he could make a quip — a joke — about someone.

"No, truly!" Psyllus said. "Why, what's a quip?"

"We great girders call it a short saying of a sharp wit, with a bitter sense in a sweet word," Manes said.

"Girders" are "scoffers and scorning critics." They insult people.

Some words that seem sweet can be bitter. Benjamin Franklin once ended a letter (that he never sent) in this way:

"*You and I were long Friends: You are now my Enemy, and I am*

"*Yours,*"

followed by his signature.

"How can thou thus divine, divide, define, dispute, and all so suddenly?" Psyllus asked.

"Wit will have its swing: It will go where it wants to go," Manes said. "I am bewitched, inspired, inflamed, infected."

"Well, then I will not tempt thy gibing spirit," Psyllus said.

Manes said:

"Do not, Psyllus, for thy dull head will be but a grindstone for my quick wit, which if thou whet and sharpen with repartee and contradictions, *perjisti, actum est de te.*"

The Latin means: "Thou have perished; thou are finished."

Manes continued:

"I have drawn blood at someone's brains with a bitter bob — a bitter taunt."

"Let me cross myself: for I will die if I cross — contradict — thee," Psyllus said.

Characters in English Renaissance plays tend to be English, even when they are ancient Greeks. Here, Psyllus makes the sign of the cross three centuries before Jesus.

"Let me do my business, I myself am afraid lest my wit should wax warm, and then it must necessarily consume some hard head with fine and pretty jests," Manes said. "I am sometimes in such a vein — such a mood — that for lack of some dull head to work on, I begin to gird and taunt myself."

"May the gods shield me from such a fine fellow, whose words melt wits like wax," Psyllus said.

"Well, then let us get to the matter," Manes said. "In faith, my master means tomorrow to fly."

That was the topic of the proclamation: Diogenes would fly the next day.

"It is a jest," Psyllus said. "You are joking."

"Is it a jest to fly?" Manes said. "If thou were to fly in jest, soon thou would repent it in earnest."

Flying is serious business.

"Well, I will be the cryer," Psyllus said.

Manes cried, "Oyez! Oyez! Oyez! All manner of men, women, or children, who will come tomorrow into the marketplace, between the hours of nine and ten, shall see Diogenes the Cynic fly."

"Oyez" means: "Pay attention. Hear what I have to say."

Psyllus cried:

"Oyez! Oyez! Oyez! All manner of men, women, or children, who will come tomorrow into the marketplace, between the hours of nine and ten, shall see Diogenes the Cynic —"

He did not finish the proclamation, but said:

"I do not think he will fly."

"Bah, say 'fly,'" Manes said.

"Fly," Psyllus said.

"Now let us go," Manes said, "for I will not see him again until midnight. I have a back way into his tub."

"Which way do thou call the back way, when every way is open?" Psyllus said.

"I mean to come in at his back," Manes said.

Hmm. Indelicate, that.

"Well, let us go away, so that we may return speedily," Psyllus said.

They exited.

— 3.3 —

Apelles and Campaspe talked together in Apelles' art studio.

"I shall never draw your eyes well because they blind mine," Apelles said.

"Why then, paint me without eyes, for I am blind," Campaspe said.

She was going into art modeling blind: without knowing what she was doing. She had never been painted before.

Art modeling does require skill: Models have to remain motionless for long periods of time.

Love, however, is blind, as is Cupid. Campaspe may be in love.

"Were you ever shadowed — painted — before by anyone?" Apelles asked.

"No," Campaspe said, "And I wish that you could so now shadow me that I might not be perceived by anyone."

"Shadow" can mean "paint," but Campaspe was saying that she wanted to be hidden by being in shadows.

"It would be a pity if so absolutely perfect a face should not furnish Venus' temple among these pictures," Apelles said.

Apelles painted beautiful women and goddesses. It would be a pity if Campaspe's portrait were not among the other portraits of beauties whom Apelles had painted.

"What are these pictures?" Campaspe asked.

"This is Leda, whom Jove deceived while he was in the likeness of a swan," Apelles said.

"A fair woman, but a foul deceit," Campaspe said.

Leda was a beautiful woman, and Jupiter committed a foul — and fowl — deceit.

"This is Alcmena, unto whom Jupiter came in the shape of Amphitrion, her husband, and begat Hercules," Apelles said.

"A famous son, but an infamous deed," Campaspe said.

When Alcmena slept with Jupiter, she thought that she was sleeping with her husband.

In Homer's *Odyssey*, Odysseus (his Roman name is Ulysses) talked to his wife, Penelope, after he killed all the suitors who had plagued her. Penelope had been waiting for her husband to return home for twenty years, and she did not want to make a mistake and sleep with the wrong man, or with a shape-shifting god. Odysseus proved that he was her husband by revealing his knowledge of their bed.

Penelope tried to trick Odysseus by telling a servant to bring out the bed that she and her husband shared, and Odysseus said:

"First I built my bedroom over the olive tree, and then I trimmed the olive tree to make a post for our bed. After I built the bed, I finished the rest of my palace. This is our secret sign, Penelope. No one should know about that bed. Not even the gods know about it — they can't see through the walls and roof that I built before I built our bed.

"Penelope, is our bed still deeply rooted, or has a man been in the bedroom to cut the roots of our bed — and our marriage?"

Of course, the bed was still deeply rooted, and the bed is an important symbol of their deeply rooted marriage.

"He might do it because he was a god," Apelles said.

If might makes right, then whatever the gods do is right because they are mighty.

"Nay, therefore it was evilly done, because he was a god," Campaspe said.

Campaspe believed that the gods ought to obey a very strict moral code, but the ancient Greek and Roman gods were entirely capable of rape.

"This is Danae, into whose prison Jupiter drizzled a golden shower, and obtained his desire," Apelles said, showing another painting.

Danae bore Jupiter a son: the hero Perseus.

"What gold can make one yield to desire?" Campaspe asked.

"This is Europa, whom Jupiter ravished," Apelles said. "And this is Antiopa."

In a shape of a satyr, Jupiter raped Antiopa, who bore him a son: Amphion, who helped build the walls of Thebes by playing music. Stones rose from the ground and fitted themselves into their positions in the walls without any other help than the music. Amphion had a twin brother, Zethus, whose father was mortal.

"Were all the gods like this Jupiter?" Campaspe asked.

"There were many gods like this Jupiter," Apelles said.

"I think in those days love was well ratified and sanctioned among men on earth, when lust was so fully authorized by the gods in Heaven," Campaspe said.

"Nay, you may imagine there were women surpassingly amiable and worthy to be loved, when there were exceedingly amorous gods," Apelles said.

"If women were never so fair, men would be false," Campaspe said.

"If women were never so false, men would be fond: amorous and foolish," Apelles said.

"Never so" can mean "especially."

"What counterfeit [What painting] is this, Apelles?" Campaspe asked.

"This is Venus, the goddess of love," Apelles said.

"What! Are there also loving goddesses?" Campaspe asked.

"This is she who has power to command the very affections of the heart," Apelles said.

"How is she hired and engaged for services: by prayer, by sacrifice, or by bribes?" Campaspe asked.

"By prayer, by sacrifice, and by bribes," Apelles said.

"What prayer?" Campaspe asked.

"Vows irrevocable," Apelles said.

"What sacrifice?" Campaspe asked.

"Hearts ever sighing, never dissembling," Apelles said.

"What bribes?" Campaspe asked.

"Roses and kisses, but were you never in love?" Apelles asked.

"No, nor was love ever in me," Campaspe said.

A person with a bawdy mind might think she had said, "No, nor was Love ever in me."

"Love" with a capital L is Cupid.

"Then you have injured many!" Apelles said.

"How so?" Campaspe asked.

"Because you have been loved by many," Apelles said.

"I have been flattered perhaps by some," Campaspe said.

"It is not possible that a face so fair, and a wit so sharp, both without comparison, should not be apt to love," Apelles said.

"If you begin to tip your tongue with cunning, I ask you to dip your pencil [your fine, tapered paintbrush] in colors," Campaspe said, "and I ask you to fall to that which you must do, not that which you wish to do."

Clitus and Parmenio, who were officers in Alexander the Great's army, talked together in the palace.

Clitus said, "Parmenio, I cannot tell how it comes to pass that in Alexander nowadays there grows an impatient kind of life. In the morning he is melancholy, and at noon he is solemn. At all times he is either more sour or more severe than he was accustomed to be."

Parmenio replied, "In kings' cases I prefer to doubt rather than conjecture, and I think it is better to be ignorant than inquisitive. Kings have long ears and long stretched-out arms, and in the heads of kings suspicion is a proof, and to be accused is to be condemned."

In other words: Kings have spies, and kings are overly suspicious, and so it is better not to know things that can get you in trouble with a king.

A being with long ears — an ass — can misinterpret things.

Clitus said, "Yet between us there can be no danger to find out the cause of Alexander's moods because we have no ill will that would make us reject a plausible explanation, such as these three:

"First, it may be an unquenchable thirst of conquering that makes Alexander unquiet.

"Second, it is not unlikely that his long ease here in Athens has altered his mood and character.

"Third, it is not impossible that he should be in love."

Parmenio said:

"In love, Clitus?

"No, no, it is as far from his thought as treason is in ours.

"Alexander, whose always-waking eye, whose never-tired heart, whose body patient of labor, whose mind insatiable of victory has always been noted, cannot so soon be melted into the weak fancies of love.

"Aristotle told him there were many worlds, and Alexander, who longs to conquer all worlds, galls because he has not conquered even one world.

"But here he comes."

Alexander the Great and Hephestion entered the scene.

Alexander the Great said, "Parmenio and Clitus, I want you both to be ready to go into Persia on an embassage no less profitable to me than honorable to yourselves."

Alexander had not forgotten about his desire for conquest.

"We are ready for all commands," Clitus said. "We wish nothing else, but continually to be commanded."

Alexander the Great said:

"Well, then withdraw yourselves until I have further considered about this matter."

Clitus and Parmenio exited.

Alexander the Great then said:

"Now we will see how Apelles goes forward: I fear that nature has overcome art, and her countenance has overcome his cunning."

In other words: I am afraid that Campaspe is too beautiful for Apelles to capture her beauty in paint.

"You love, and therefore think anything," Hephestion said.

"But I am not so far in love with Campaspe as I am with Bucephalus, if the opportunity arises either of conflict or of conquest," Alexander the Great said.

In the paragraph above, Bucephalus, Alexander's war horse, is figuratively warfare and conquest.

Bucephalus was a beautiful horse, but no one could ride him. Alexander noticed that Bucephalus was afraid of its own shadow. Alexander therefore had the horse face the sun as he trained it. Soon, Bucephalus lost its fear of its own shadow.

"Occasion cannot be lacking, if will is not lacking," Hephestion said.

In other words: If Alexander has the will to fight and conquer, he will not lack the opportunity to fight and conquer.

Hephestion said:

"Behold all Persia, which is swelling in the pride of its own power.

"Behold the Scythians, who are unworried about what courage or fortune can do to them."

Alexander had both much courage and much good fortune, aka much good luck.

Hephestion said:

"Behold the Egyptians, who are dreaming in the soothsayings of their augurs, and gaping over the smoke of their beasts' entrails."

Augurs revealed the will of the gods. As a form of soothsaying, augurs would kill animals and examine their entrails.

In Book 1 of Homer's *Iliad*, a plague fell on the Greeks after Agamemnon took a spear-bride who was the daughter of a priest of Apollo. Agamemnon then refused a ransom for the priest's daughter.

At a meeting that Achilles, the best warrior in the Trojan War, called, the soothsayer Chalchas revealed the cause of the plague:

"Apollo is not angry at us because of a lack of sacrifice or a vow that we failed to fulfill. Instead, the god is angry because of the actions of Agamemnon. The priest of Apollo acted correctly when he tried to ransom his daughter, but Agamemnon disrespected the old priest. Agamemnon should have respected the old priest and the god — Apollo — the priest serves. Now, because of Agamemnon's disrespect to him, Apollo shoots his arrows at us and kills us with plague. The deaths will not stop until we give the old priest his daughter — without taking shining treasure as ransom. She must be given back to her father with no price paid for her freedom. Both she and a hundred bulls need to be sent to the city of Chryse; the bulls must be sacrificed to Apollo. Only then will Apollo be appeased and stop the killing."

Spear-brides are among the spoils of war. Warriors who fought well would be awarded with treasure, animals, and women. A young, pretty woman would become a spear-bride, aka sex-slave.

Campaspe was among the spoils of war, and she became a slave. Earlier, however, Alexander gave her and other slaves their freedom. In history, Campaspe was Alexander's favorite concubine. He had sex with her, but he was not married to her.

Hephestion continued:

"All these, Alexander, are to be subdued, if that world has not slipped out of your head, that world which you have sworn to conquer with that hand."

As they talked, they walked to the marketplace, where Diogenes the Cynic and his tub were located.

Alexander the Great said:

"I confess the labor's fit for Alexander, and yet recreation is necessary among so many assaults, bloody wounds, and intolerable troubles. Give me a little time, if not to sit, yet to breathe and catch my breath. And don't doubt that Alexander can, when he will, throw affections as far from him as he can cowardice.

"But behold Diogenes talking with someone at his tub."

Crysus, a beggar, asked Diogenes for money: "One penny, Diogenes. I am a Cynic."

"He who first gave thee anything made thee a beggar," Diogenes said.

"Why, if thou will give nothing, nobody will give thee anything," Crysus said.

"I lack nothing, until the springs dry, and the earth perish," Diogenes said.

"I gather for the gods," Crysus said.

"And I don't care for those gods who lack money and want money," Diogenes said.

"Thou who will give nothing are not a true Cynic," Crysus said.

"Thou who will beg anything are not a true Cynic," Diogenes said.

He went back inside his tub.

"Alexander, King Alexander, give a poor Cynic a groat," Crysus said.

A groat is a small amount of money.

"It is not for a king to give a groat," Alexander the Great said.

"Then give me a talent," Crysus said.

A talent is a large amount of money.

Alexander the Great said:

"It is not for a beggar to ask for a talent.

"Go away!"

Crysus exited.

Alexander the Great and Hephestion went to the art studio in which were Apelles and Campaspe and stood in front of it.

Alexander the Great then called, "Apelles."

"Here I am," Apelles said.

Campaspe was with him.

Alexander the Great said to her, "Now, gentlewoman, doesn't your beauty put the painter to his trump?"

To paint Campaspe, Apelles must put forth his best effort: He must play his trump card.

Modestly, Campaspe said, "Yes, my lord. Seeing so disordered a countenance [face], he fears he shall shadow [paint] a deformed counterfeit."

Campaspe went back inside the art studio.

Alexander the Great said to himself:

"I wish that he could color the life — her personality — along with painting the features."

He then said:

"And I think, Apelles, if you were as cunning as report says you are, you may paint flowers as well with sweet smells as fresh colors, observing in your mixture of paint such things as should draw near to their savors — their scents."

"Your majesty must know that it is no less hard to paint savors, than virtues; colors can neither speak nor think," Apelles said.

"Where do you first begin when you draw any picture?" Alexander the Great asked.

"The face in as just compass and proper proportion as I can," Apelles said.

"I would begin with the eye, as a light to all the rest," Alexander the Great said.

"If you will paint, since you are a king, your majesty may begin where you please; but as you would be a painter, you must begin with the face," Apelles said.

Kings can do whatever they want; good painters must do what will result in a good painting.

"Aurelius would in one hour color four faces," Alexander the Great said.

"I marvel that he did not color four faces in half an hour," Apelles said.

"Why? Is it so easy?" Alexander the Great asked.

"No, but he does it so homely and so roughly: His work is unsophisticated, and so he can work fast."

"When will you finish Campaspe?" Alexander the Great asked.

"I will never finish her portrait, for always in absolute beauty there is something above the ability of art to capture it," Apelles said.

"Why shouldn't I by labor and practice be as skillful as you, Apelles?" Alexander the Great asked.

Apelles answered, "May God forbid that you should have cause to be as skillful as Apelles!"

"I think four colors are sufficient to shadow any countenance, and so it was in the time of Phydias," Alexander the Great said.

Some ancient Greek painters used only four colors to complete their paintings: black, red, yellow, and white.

Apelles said:

"Then men had fewer fancies, and women had not as many favors."

Modern women — that is, the women of Apelles' day — were much more fashion-conscious and used more colors in their makeup and clothing than ancient women did.

Apelles continued:

"Nowadays, if the hair of her eyebrows is black, the hair of her head must yet be yellow.

"The attire of her head must be different from the clothing of her body, else the picture would seem like the blazon — a painted coat of arms — of ancient armory, not like the sweet delight of newly found amiableness and beauty.

"Just as in elaborate flower beds, a diversity of odors makes a sweeter scent, or as in music a diversity of strings causes a more delicate harmony and accord, so in painting, the more colors, the better counterfeit, observing black for a background and foundation, and the rest for grace."

"Lend me thy charcoal-pencil, Apelles. I will color, and thou shall judge my work," Alexander the Great said.

A charcoal-pencil is a piece of charcoal used for drawing.

"Here," Apelles said.

"The coal breaks," Alexander the Great said.

"You press too hard," Apelles said.

"Now it does not make a black mark," Alexander the Great said.

"You press too soft," Apelles said.

"This is awry," Alexander the Great said.

"Your eye goes not with your hand," Apelles said.

Alexander's eye and hand were not working together.

"Now it is worse," Alexander the Great said.

"Your hand goes not with your mind," Apelles said.

Alexander's hand and mind were not working together.

Alexander the Great said:

"Nay, if all is too hard or too soft, and if there are so many rules and regards, and if one's hand, one's eye, and one's mind must all draw together, then I would rather be arranging troops for a battle than blotting a board.

"But how have I done here?"

"Like a king," Apelles said.

Alexander the Great said:

"I think so, but nothing could be more unlike a painter.

"Well, Apelles, the portrait of Campaspe is finished as I wish, so dismiss her as your model, and bring immediately her counterfeit [painted portrait] after me."

"I will," Apelles said.

Alexander the Great and Hephestion walked out of the studio.

"Now Hephestion, doesn't this matter cotton and succeed as I wish?" Alexander the Great said. "Campaspe looks pleasantly, liberty will increase her beauty, and my love shall advance her honor."

"I will not contradict your majesty, for time must wear out that which love has wrought, and reason must wean that which appetite has nursed," Hephestion said.

Wean? Nursed? Hephestion was subtly calling Alexander's judgment immature.

Campaspe walked out of the studio.

Alexander the Great said, "How stately she passes by, yet how soberly! A sweet consent in her countenance is paired with a chaste disdain, desire is mingled with coyness and shyness, and I cannot tell what to call it, but she has a curst yielding modesty!"

In other words: Campaspe is beautiful and calm with good judgment. She appears to be soft and yielding, but she also has a determined will that keeps her from doing wrong.

"Let her pass," Hephestion said.

He wanted Campaspe to pass out of Alexander's life.

"So she shall for the fairest on the earth," Alexander the Great said.

Campaspe could pass for — be regarded as — the most beautiful woman on earth.

They exited.

— 3.5 —

Psyllus and Manes walked together to Apelles' art studio and stood in front of it.

"I shall be hanged for tarrying so long," Psyllus said.

Psyllus and Manes had been proclaiming that Diogenes would fly the next day.

"I pray God my master has not flown before I come," Manes said.

This is ambiguous:

1) I hope that my master will not have flown in the sky before I get there.

2) I hope that my master will not have departed hastily before I get there.

"Leave, Manes! My master is coming," Psyllus said.

Manes exited.

Apelles came outside from his studio.

"Where have you been all this while?" Apelles asked.

"Nowhere but here," Psyllus said.

"Who has been here since I went inside my studio?" Apelles asked.

"Nobody," Psyllus said.

"Ungracious wag — foolish boy! I perceive you have been loitering. Was Alexander nobody?" Apelles said.

"He was a king," Psyllus said. "I meant no mean body."

A mean body is a person whose parents are from a mean — low — social class.

"I will beat your body with a cudgel for it, and then I will say it was 'nobody,' because it was no honest body. Go inside!" Apelles said.

Psyllus exited.

Alone, Apelles, who was in love with Campaspe, said to himself:

"Unfortunate Apelles, and therefore unfortunate because you are Apelles!

"Have thou by drawing her beauty brought to pass that thou can scarcely draw thine own breath? And by so much the more have thou increased thy concerns and worries, by how much the more thou have showed thy cunning artistic skill.

"Wasn't it sufficient to behold the fire and warm thee, but with Satyrus thou must kiss the fire and burn thyself?"

51

A satyr — a half-man, half-goat creature — saw a fire and wanted to hug and kiss it, but Prometheus warned him not to because he would be burned.

Apelles continued:

"O Campaspe, Campaspe, art must yield to nature, reason must yield to appetite, wisdom must yield to affection.

"Could Pygmalion entreat by prayer to have his ivory turned into flesh, and yet Apelles cannot obtain by lamentations to have the picture of his love changed to life?"

Alexander the Great loved the living Campaspe, and so Apelles was hoping that Venus would turn his painting of Campaspe into a second living Campaspe.

Apelles continued:

"Is painting portraits so far inferior to carving sculpture? Or do thou, Venus, more delight to be hewed with chisels, than shadowed with colors?

"What Pygmalion, or what Pyrgoteles, or what Lysippus is he who ever made thy face as fair as I, or spread thy fame as far as I? Perhaps thou, Venus, in this envy my art, thinking that in coloring my sweet Campaspe, I have left no place by cunning and skill to make thee as amiable and beautiful as I made Campaspe."

Perhaps Apelles had already created his masterpiece, and now he could not paint as well as he had painted Campaspe.

Pygmalion, Pyrgoteles, and Lysippus were all sculptors, and Pyrgoteles was also a gem-cutter.

Pygmalion carved a marble statue of a beautiful woman, and he fell in love with it. He prayed to Venus to make the statue living flesh, Venus granted his prayer, and Pygmalion and the live woman (and former statue) lived together happily ever after.

Apelles continued:

"But alas! She is the paramour to a prince. Alexander the monarch of the earth has both her body and her affection. For what is it that kings cannot obtain by prayers, threats, and promises?

"Won't she think it better to sit under a cloth of estate — the canopy over the throne — like a queen, than in a poor shop like a housewife? And won't she esteem it sweeter to be the concubine of the lord of the world, than the spouse to a painter in Athens?

"Yes, yes, Apelles, thou may swim against the stream with the crab, and feed against the wind with the deer, and peck against the steel with the cockatrice."

It is easier to swim downstream than upstream.

Deer are safer when the wind blows toward them the scent of their enemy.

A cockatrice, aka a basilisk, was a half-cock, half-serpent mythological creature whose look could kill. If it looked into a mirror, it would die.

Apelles continued:

"Stars are to be looked at, not reached at. Princes are to be yielded unto, not contended with. Campaspe is to be honored, not obtained, and she is to be painted, not possessed by thee.

"O fair face! O unhappy hand! And why did thou draw so fair a face?"

The beautiful face belonged to Campaspe; the unhappy hand belonged to Apelles, who had painted Campaspe's beautiful face.

Apelles continued:

"O beautiful countenance, the express image of Venus, but somewhat fresher: She is the only example of that eternity, which Jupiter dreaming of asleep, could not conceive again once he awakened."

Campaspe was so beautiful that Jupiter can only dream of her.

Apelles continued:

"Blush, Venus, for I am ashamed to finish my painting of thee.

"Now I must paint things impossible for my level of skill, but agreeable with my emotions. I must paint deep and hollow sighs, sad and melancholy thoughts, wounds and slaughters of my imagination. I must paint a life posting to death, a death galloping from life, a wavering constancy, an unsettled resolution, and what but these must I paint, Apelles?

"But as they who are shaken with a fever are to be warmed with clothes, not with groans, and as he who melts away in a consumption is to be cured by cullices [by medicinal broths], not by conceits [not by daydreams], so the feeding canker — destructive caterpillar — of my care and anxiety, the never dying worm of my heart, is to be killed by counsel and advice, not by cries, and by the applying of remedies, not by the replying of reasons.

"And since in desperate cases, there must be used medicines that are extreme, I will hazard that little life which is left to me to restore the greater part that is lost, and this shall be my first plan and medicine, for wit and intelligence must work where authority is not.

"As soon as Alexander has viewed this portrait, I will by a ruse give it a blemish, so by that means she may come again to my shop and model for me so I can repair the blemish; and then it would be as good to utter my love, and die with denial, as to conceal it, and live in despair.

Apelles then sang this song:

"Cupid and my Campaspe played

"At cards for kisses, Cupid paid;

"He stakes his quiver, bow, and arrows,

"His mother's doves, and team of sparrows;

"Loses them, too; then, down he throws

"The coral of his lip, the rose

"Growing on's [on his] cheek (but none knows how),

"With these, the crystal of his brow,

"And then the dimple of his chin:

"All these did my Campaspe win.

"At last, he set [bet] her both his eyes;

"She won, and Cupid blind did rise.

"O Love! Has she done this to thee?

"What shall (Alas!) become of me?"

Campaspe is a good card player. She wins, and Cupid pays.

CHAPTER 4

— 4.1 —

It was the next day: the day that Diogenes was supposed to fly.

Solinus, Psyllus, and Granichus talked together in the marketplace, near Diogenes' tub. Solinus was a citizen of Athens.

"This is the place, the day, and the time that Diogenes has appointed that he will fly," Solinus said. "This is something I will not miss witnessing!"

"I will not lose the opportunity to see the flight of so fair a fowl as Diogenes is, even if my master would beat with a cudgel my 'nobody,' as he threatened earlier," Psyllus said.

When Psyllus takes an unpermitted leave of absence, he is a nobody, as in, "Nobody is here where Psyllus is supposed to be."

"What, Psyllus? Will the beast wag his wings today?" Granichus asked.

Psyllus said:

"We shall hear, for here comes Manes."

He called:

"Manes, will it be? Will it happen?"

Manes walked over to him.

He said, "Be! It would be best for him to be as cunning as a bee, or else shortly he will not be at all."

"How is he equipped to fly?" Granichus asked. "Has he feathers?"

"Thou are an ass! Capons, geese, and owls have feathers," Manes said.

Capons are associated with cuckolds, geese are associated with fools, and owls are associated with bad omens.

Manes continued:

"He has found Daedalus' old waxen wings, and he has been piecing them — mending and enlarging them — this month, because he is so broad in the shoulders."

By the way, the name "Plato" is actually a nickname meaning "broad." Some people think that he was broad in the shoulders. Some people joke that he was fat.

Daedalus was an inventor, and he created the labyrinth in which the Minotaur, whose mother was Pasiphae, was kept.

Pasiphae was guilty of bestiality: having sex with an animal. She was a Queen of Crete who fell in love with a bull, so she commissioned Daedalus to create an artificial cow for her to creep into. The bull had sex with the artificial cow (and with Pasiphae), and Pasiphae conceived and gave birth to the Minotaur, a mythical half-human, half-bull creature that feasted on human flesh. After Pasiphae gave birth to the Minotaur, Daedalus built the labyrinth that housed the Minotaur.

Androgeos, the son of King Minos and Queen Pasiphae of Crete, competed in athletic contests against Athenian athletes and won, but the Athenian losers were jealous of his victories and murdered him. As a result of the murder, King Minos demanded that the Athenians periodically pay a tribute to Crete of young men and young women. These young people were put in the labyrinth, and the Minotaur killed them and feasted on their bodies.

Eventually, Theseus of Athens arrived to kill the Minotaur. Ariadne, the daughter of King Minos, helped him by giving him a spool of string that Theseus used to get out of the maze after he had killed the Minotaur.

Because Daedalus had given Ariadne the idea of the spool of string, he was imprisoned with his son, Icarus, and he fashioned wings made out of wax and feathers so that they could fly away from the island where they were imprisoned. He warned his son not to fly too high, for if he did, the sun would melt the wax, the feathers would fall out of the wings, and he would fall into the sea and drown.

This is exactly what happened. Icarus became excited because he was flying, he flew too high, the wax of his wings melted, the feathers fell out of the wings, and he drowned.

Manes continued:

"O you shall see him cut the air even like a tortoise."

A fable told about a tortoise that two cranes tried to help find new water. The cranes held the ends of a stick in their mouths, and the tortoise held onto the stick with its teeth. The cranes warned the tortoise not to speak, but the tortoise heard some villagers laughing at him as he was high in the air. Angry, the tortoise opened his mouth to insult the villagers, and he fell.

"I think that so wise a man should not be so mad," Solinus said. "His body must necessarily be too heavy to fly."

"Why, he has eaten nothing this week but cork and feathers," Manes said.

Psyllus whispered to Manes, "Touch him, Manes."

A touch in fencing scores a point. Psyllus wanted Manes to score a point against Solinus by telling him a tall tale.

"He is so light that he can scarcely keep himself from flying at midnight," Manes said.

Witches and birds of ill omen fly at midnight.

Many people entered the scene, hoping to see Diogenes fly.

"See, they begin to flock, and look, my master bustles himself to fly," Manes said.

Diogenes came out of his tub.

He berated the crowd members:

"You wicked and bewitched Athenians, whose bodies make the earth groan, and whose breaths infect the air with stench.

"Did you come to see Diogenes fly? Diogenes comes to see you sink.

"You call me 'Dog,' and so I am, for I long to gnaw the bones in your skins.

"You call me a hater of men. No, I am a hater of your way of life. Your dissolute lives, not fearing death, will prove your desperate deaths, not hoping for life after death."

In Christian despair, people lose their hope for salvation and life after death.

Diogenes continued:

"What else do you do in Athens but sleep in the day, and surfeit — overindulge — in the night? You are back gods in the morning with pride, and in the evening you are belly gods with gluttony!"

By "back gods," Diogenes may simply mean that they lie on their back as they oversleep.

Proud backs don't bend, and people lying on their backs in bed have straight backs.

Diogenes continued:

"You flatter kings, and call them gods. Now speak the truth about yourselves, and confess you are devils!

"From the bee you have not taken the honey, but you have taken the wax to make your religion, framing it to the time, not to the truth."

Wax is malleable: It can be shaped. The Athenians are molding their religion to suit their desires. Think of prosperity theology, where the focus is on getting wealth for yourself, not on helping other people. Who is more likely to be a good Christian? A Franciscan monk who has taken a vow of poverty? Or a preacher who has a private jet?

But let's acknowledge the alternative prosperity wisdom of John Wesley, who advised Christians: "Get all you can. Save all you can. Give all you can."

Diogenes said:

"Your filthy lust you color — you disguise — under a courtly color of love, and injuries abroad you color under the title of policies at home."

In other words: Athenians commit crimes abroad, but at home they call them justified political maneuvers.

Diogenes continued:

"And secret malice creeps under the name of public justice."

In the USA, politicians pass laws that show a hatred of women, but they justify the laws by saying that they are protecting the rights of a clump of cells.

Diogenes continued:

"You have caused Alexander to dry up springs and plant vines, to sow rocket [an edible plant reputed to be an aphrodisiac] and weed endif [endive], to shear sheep and enshrine foxes."

Among other things, the Athenians prefer wine to water. They prefer sophistication to lack of sophistication. They also like to take advantage of the innocent and to make heroes of manipulators.

Diogenes continued:

"All conscience is seeled at Athens."

Falcons had their eyes seeled — sewn shut — to facilitate their training.

Diogenes continued:

"Swearing comes from a hot mettle, aka character.

"Lying comes from a quick wit.

"Flattery comes from a flowing tongue.

"Undecent talk comes from a merry disposition.

"All things are lawful at Athens.

"Either you think there are no gods, or I must think you are no men.

"You build as though you should live forever, and you surfeit — overindulge — as though you should die tomorrow.

"No one teaches 'true philosophy' except Aristotle, because he was the king's schoolmaster!"

According to Diogenes, Aristotle gets a good reputation as a philosopher because he associates with Alexander.

Diogenes continued:

"O times! O men! O corruption in manners!"

Cicero also decried the state of the society and the men in his time.

Diogenes continued:

"Remember that green grass must turn to dry hay.

"When you sleep, you are not sure to wake again, and when you rise, you are not certain to lie down again (because you may die in the meantime).

"Look never so high — your heads must lie level with your feet. Thus have I flown over and surveyed your disordered lives, and if you will not amend your manners, I will study to fly further from you, so that I may be nearer to honesty."

"Thou rave, Diogenes, for thy life is different from thy words," Solinus said. "Didn't I see thee come out of a brothel house? Wasn't that a shame?"

"It was no shame to go out, but it was a shame to go in," Diogenes said.

"It would be a good deed, Manes, to beat thy master," Granichus said.

"It would be as good a deed for you to eat my master," Manes said.

One of the people in the crowd asked, "Have thou made us all fools, and will thou not fly?"

"I tell thee, unless thou be honest," Diogenes said. "I will fly."

He would flee from Athens because it was so corrupt.

People in the crowd shouted, "Dog! Dog! Take a bone!"

"Thy father need fear no dogs, but dogs need fear thy father," Diogenes said.

People in the crowd shouted, "We will tell Alexander that thou reprove him behind his back."

"And I will tell him that you flatter him before his face," Diogenes said.

People in the crowd shouted, "We will cause all the boys in the street to hiss in disapproval at thee."

"Indeed, I think the Athenians have their children ready for any vice because they are Athenians," Diogenes said.

"Why, master, do you intend not to fly?" Manes asked.

"No, Manes, not without wings," Diogenes said.

He meant biological wings, not the wings of Daedalus.

"Everybody will account you a liar," Manes said.

"No, I promise you they won't, for I will always say that the Athenians are evil," Diogenes said.

If Diogenes tells the truth — that the Athenians are evil — he ought not to be called a liar.

"I don't care," Psyllus said. "It was entertainment enough for me to see these old huddles hit home."

Diogenes had thoroughly insulted the old huddles: the people in the crowd. And they had thoroughly insulted him.

"Nor do I care," Granichus said.

"Come, let us go!" Psyllus said. "And hereafter whenever I intend to rail upon and criticize any crowd of people openly, it shall be given out that I will fly."

He would imitate Diogenes by announcing that he would fly, and after a crowd of people had gathered, he would denounce them.

They exited.

Campaspe was alone in a room in Apelles' house.

She said to herself:

"Campaspe, it is hard to judge whether thy choice is more unwise, or thy chance — thy luck and fortune — is more unfortunate.

"Do thou prefer — but wait, don't utter in words that which makes thine ears glow with thoughts.

"Bah! It's better that thy tongue wag than thy heart break! Has a painter crept further into thy mind than a prince? Has Apelles crept further into thy mind than Alexander?

"Fond, foolish wench! The baseness of thy mind betrays the meanness of thy birth.

"But alas! Passionate love is a fire, which kindles as well in the bramble as in the oak; and it catches hold where it first alights, not where it may best burn.

"Larks that climb aloft in the air build their nests below on the earth; and women who cast their eyes upon kings may place their hearts upon vassals. A needle will become thy fingers better than a lute, and a distaff is fitter for thy hand than a scepter.

"Ants live safely, until they have gotten wings, and juniper is not blown up until it has gotten a high top."

Small shrubs bend in hard winds and survive; tall trees don't bend and are blown down.

Campaspe continued:

"The people of a low and mean estate are without worry and anxiety as long as they continue to be without pride.

"But here comes Apelles, in whom I wish there were the like love and affection for me that I have for him."

Apelles entered the scene.

He said, "Gentlewoman, the misfortune I had with your picture will put you to some pains to sit again to be painted."

The "misfortune" was the deliberate "accident" that resulted in a blemish on the picture.

"It is small pains for me to sit still, but infinite for you to draw still — to draw continually," Campaspe said.

"No, madam! To paint Venus was a pleasure, but to shadow [paint] the sweet face of Campaspe is a heaven!" Apelles said.

Campaspe said, "If your tongue were made of the same flesh that your heart is, your words would be as your thoughts are, but it is such a common thing among all you men to commend that often for fashion's sake you call them beautiful whom you know are black and ugly."

In other words: Apelles' words do not match his thoughts.

This culture regarded white skin as more beautiful than black skin.

"What might men do to be believed?" Apelles asked.

"Whet their tongues on their hearts," Campaspe said.

The *Oxford English Dictionary* defines "whet" as "Something that incites or stimulates desire; an incitement or inducement to action," but the first recorded use is in 1698.

If their tongues were in conformity with their heartfelt thoughts and emotions, as they would be if their tongues were stimulated with the love that is in their hearts, men would say what they think.

"So they do, and they speak as they think," Apelles said.

"I wish they did!" Campaspe said.

Campaspe wanted Apelles to say that he loved her.

"I wish they didn't!" Apelles said.

Apelles believed that his love for Campaspe was hopeless because Alexander the Great was his rival for her love, and so he did not want to say he loved her.

"Why, would you have them dissemble?" Campaspe asked.

"Not in love, but their love," Apelles said.

A loving couple ought not to dissemble to each other, but in such a situation as Apelles found himself in, where his love was hopeless, he did not want to reveal his love.

Apelles then asked, "But will you give me permission to ask you a question without offence?"

"As long as you will answer another question for me without excuse," Campaspe said.

"Whom do you love best in the world?" Apelles asked.

"He who made me last in the world," Campaspe said.

"That was a god," Apelles said.

God created Eve after he had created Adam.

"I had thought it had been a man," Campaspe said.

Apelles had made a portrait of her.

Campaspe then asked, "But whom do you honor most, Apelles?"

"The thing that is most like you, Campaspe," Apelles said.

"My picture?" Campaspe asked.

"I dare not venture upon your person," Apelles said. "But come, let us go in, for Alexander will think it a long time until we return."

They went into the art studio.

Clitus and Parmenio talked together in a room in the palace.

Earlier, Alexander the Great had ordered them to be prepared to undertake an embassage. Alexander the Great had said, "Parmenio and Clitus, I want you both to be ready to go into Persia on an embassage no less profitable to me than honorable to yourselves."

But now Clitus said:

"We hear nothing about our embassage, which was a pretext perhaps to blear our eyes, or tickle our ears, or inflame our hearts."

In other words: The talk about an embassage was perhaps simply a pretext to keep Clitus and Parmenio from being impatient about Alexander's stay in Athens because they would think that Alexander was planning an excursion into Persia.

"But what does Alexander do in the meantime, except use for tantara, sol, fa, la; use for his hard couch, down beds; and use for his handful of water, his standing cup of wine?"

Alexander was trading the hard life of a conqueror for the soft life of a king. Instead of the tantara of military music, he was hearing the sol, fa, la of love songs. Instead of a hard bed in a military camp, he was sleeping in a down bed. Instead of drinking a handful of water on a battlefield, he was drinking lots of wine in Athens.

A standing cup is a cup with a stem and a base on which it stands.

Parmenio said:

"Clitus, I mislike this new delicacy and pleasing peace, for what else do we see now than a kind of softness in every man's mind?

"What else do we see now than bees that make their hives in soldiers' helmets because the helmets are not being used?

"What else do we see now than our steeds furnished with ornamental footcloths of gold, instead of useful saddles of steel?

"More time is required to scour the rust of our weapons than was accustomed to be used in subduing the countries of our enemies."

Weapons that are frequently used in battle have little rust.

Parmenio continued:

"Since Alexander fell from his hard armor to his soft robes, behold the face of his court:

"Youths who were accustomed to decorate their shields with images of victory, now engrave posies — short mottos — of love in their rings.

"They who were accustomed on trotting horses to charge the enemy with a lance, now in comfortable coaches ride up and down to court ladies.

"Instead of sword and shield to hazard their lives, they use pen and paper to paint their loves.

"Yes, such a fear and faintness have grown in court that they wish rather to hear the blowing of a horn calling them to hunt than the sound of a trumpet calling them to fight."

Parmenio now addressed King Philip of Macedon, who had died in 336 B.C.E.

"O Philip, if thou were alive to see this alteration — thy men turned into women, thy soldiers turned into lovers, and gloves worn in velvet caps instead of plumes worn in graven helmets — thou would either die among them out of sorrow or destroy them out of anger."

The gloves worn in velvet caps were gifts from women.

Clitus said, "Stop, Parmenio, lest in speaking what does not become thee, thou feel what thou will not like."

Parmenio was speaking words that a tyrant could interpret as being traitorous. A tyrant can punish a traitor or "traitor" with torture and death.

Clitus continued:

"Truth is never without a scratched face, whose tongue although it cannot be cut out, yet it must be tied up."

Yes, telling the truth to power can be dangerous. Clitus was advising Parmenio to metaphorically tie up his tongue.

Parmenio said:

"It grieves me not a little for Hephestion, who thirsts for honor, not ease; but such is his fortune and nearness in friendship to Alexander that he must lay a pillow under his head, when he would prefer to put a shield in his hand.

"But let us go in, in order to see how well it becomes them to tread the measures of music in a dance — them who were previously accustomed to set the order for a march."

They exited.

Apelles and Campaspe talked together in Apelles' studio. They had confessed their love for each other.

"I have now, Campaspe, almost made an end," Apelles said.

He had almost finished repairing the painting.

"You told me, Apelles, you would never end," Campaspe said.

"I shall never end my love for you, for it shall be eternal," Apelles said.

"That is, neither to have beginning nor to have ending," Campaspe said.

Scholastic philosophers defined "eternity" as "having no beginning or end." Apelles' love for Campaspe, of course, had a beginning.

"You are disposed to misinterpret what I say," Apelles said. "I hope you do not mistrust me."

"What will you say if Alexander perceives your love for me?" Campaspe asked.

"I will say it is no treason to love," Apelles said.

"But what if he will not allow thee to see my person?" Campaspe asked.

"Then I will gaze continually on thy picture," Apelles said.

"That will not feed thy heart," Campaspe said.

"Yet it shall fill my eye," Apelles said. "Besides the sweet thoughts, the sure hopes and expectations, and thy declared faith and love will cause me to embrace thy shadow [painting] continually in my arms, and by strong imagination I will make a substance [a living Campaspe] of the shadow [picture]."

He was thinking of Pygmalion, whose love for a statue brought it to life (with the assistance of the goddess Venus).

"Well, I must be gone," Campaspe said, "but assure yourself that I would rather be in thy shop, grinding colors, than in Alexander's court, following higher fortunes."

Apelles exited into his shop.

Alone, before going to Alexander's palace, Campaspe said to herself:

"Foolish wench, what have thou done?

"Thou have done that — alas! — which cannot be undone, and therefore I fear that I am undone — that I am ruined.

"But being content is such a life that I don't care for abundance."

Being with Apelles made her happy; she did not need riches.

Campaspe continued:

"O Apelles, thy love comes from the heart, but Alexander's love from the mouth.

"The love of kings is like the blowing of winds, which whistle sometimes gently among the leaves, and then quickly turn the trees up by the roots; or fire, which warms afar off, and burns near at hand; or the sea, which makes men hoist their sails in a flattering calm and makes them cut their masts in a rough storm."

Cutting the masts was a quick way to get rid of sails in strong winds that could cause the ship to capsize.

Campaspe continued:

"Kings place love and affection by times, by policy, by appointment and arrangement.

"If kings frown, who dares call them unconstant and unfaithful?

"If kings betray secrets, who will call them untrue?"

How many readers thought of Donald Trump after reading this?

Campaspe continued:

"If kings fall to other loves, who does not tremble if the kings call them unfaithful?

"In kings there can be no love, except love given to queens, for they must meet in majesty as near as they do in love and affection.

"It is necessary — it is the best policy — to stand aloof from kings' love, Jove, and lightning."

Apelles came out of his art studio.

He said to himself:

"Now, Apelles, gather thy wits together: Campaspe is no less wise than fair, and thyself must be no less cunning than faithful.

"It is no small matter to be a rival to Alexander."

Alexander's page entered the scene.

The page said, "Apelles, you must come away quickly with the picture; the king thinks that now you have painted it, you play with it."

In other words: The painting is finished. Stop tinkering with it.

"If I would play with pictures, I have enough at home," Apelles said.

"There are none perhaps you like as well," the page said.

"It may be the case that I have painted none as well as I painted this one," Apelles said.

"I have known many fairer faces than that of Campaspe," the page said.

"And I have known many better boys than you," Apelles said.

CHAPTER 5

— 5.1 —

Diogenes was in his tub in the marketplace.

Sylvius, Perim, Milo, Trico, and Manes walked over to him.

Sylvius was a citizen of Athens, and Perim, Milo, and Trico were his sons.

"I have brought my sons, Diogenes, to be taught by thee," Sylvius said.

"What can thy sons do?" Diogenes asked.

"You shall see their qualities and accomplishments," Sylvius replied.

He then said to his son Perim:

"Dance, sirrah!"

Perim danced.

Sylvius asked Diogenes, "How do you like this? Does he dance well?"

"The better, the worser," Diogenes said.

In other words: The better you dance, the worse it is for you.

Or: The better you do it, the worse you do it.

Apparently, Diogenes did not regard dancing as an activity worth pursuing.

Someone might say today: The more experienced you become at watching junk television, the worse off you are.

(But dancing is much more valuable than watching junk television.)

"The music is very good," Sylvius said.

"The musicians are very bad," Diogenes said. "They only study to have their strings in tune, never framing their way of life to order."

Diogenes believed it was more important to have one's moral life in tune than to have one's music strings in tune.

Sylvius said:

"Now you shall see the other."

He said to his son Milo:

"Tumble, sirrah!"

Milo tumbled. He was a gymnast.

Diogenes laughed.

Sylvius asked, "How do you like this? Why do you laugh?"

"I laugh to see a wag — a boy — who was born to break his neck by destiny, practice it by art," Diogenes said.

Gymnastics is a beautiful art and sport, but it is dangerous. In 1988, Julissa Gomez was paralyzed while vaulting. In 1989, Adriana Duffy was paralyzed while vaulting. In 1998, Sang Lan was paralyzed while vaulting.

"This dog will bite me," Milo said. "I will not be a student with him."

"Don't be afraid, boy: Dogs eat no thistles," Diogenes said.

Thistles are noxious and prickly, and according to Diogenes, so is Milo.

"I marvel what kind of dog thou are, if thou are a dog," Perim said.

"When I am hungry, I am a mastiff," Diogenes said, "and when my belly is full, I am a spaniel."

"Do thou believe that there are any gods, thou who are so dogged?" Sylvius asked.

"Dogged" means perverse and spiteful.

"I must necessarily believe that there are gods," Diogenes said, "for I think that thou are an enemy to them."

"Why so?" Sylvius asked.

"Because thou have taught one of thy sons to rule his legs, and not to follow learning," Diogenes said, "and thou have taught the other to bend his body every way, and his mind no way."

"Thou do nothing but snarl, and bark like a dog," Perim said.

"It is the readiest way to drive away a thief," Diogenes said.

"Now you shall hear the third, who sings like a nightingale," Sylvius said.

"I don't care, for I have a nightingale herself to sing to me," Diogenes said.

"Sing, sirrah!" Sylvius said.

Trio sang about the nightingale:

"*What bird so sings, yet so does wail?*

"*O 'tis the ravished nightingale.*"

In mythology, Procne was married to Tereus, and she bore him a son named Itys. Tereus then raped Procne's sister, Philomela, and he cut out her tongue so that she could not tell anyone what had happened. Philomela wove a tapestry that displayed pictures that told the story of the rape. When Procne saw the tapestry and realized that her husband had raped her sister, she was so angry that she killed his and her son, Itys, cooked him, and served him to her husband. When Tereus realized what she had done, he grabbed an axe and pursued Procne and Philomela in order to kill them. They prayed to the gods, and the gods changed Procne into a swallow, and they changed Philomela into a nightingale. Ovid tells this story in Book 6 of his book *Metamorphoses*.

Trio continued his song, singing about the nightingale:

"'Jug, jug, jug, jug, tereu,' she cries,

"And still her woes at midnight rise.

"Brave prick song!"

"Jug" is a representative word for one of the nightingale's song-notes.

"Tereu" is the vocative of Tereus.

"Brave prick song!" means "excellent written music!"

A folk belief states the nightingale sings as it pricks its breast against a thorn.

Trio continued his song, singing now about the lark:

"Who is't now we hear?

"None but the lark so shrill and clear;

"How at Heaven's gates she claps her wings,

"The morn not waking till she sings."

Trio continued his song, singing now about the robin:

"Hark, hark, with what a pretty throat

"Poor robin red-breast tunes his note;"

Trio continued his song, singing now about the cuckoo:

"Hark how the jolly cuckoos sing

"Cuckoo, to welcome in the spring;

"Cuckoo, to welcome in the spring."

"Lo, Diogenes! I am sure thou cannot do as much as my son can," Sylvius said.

Diogenes, who knew he could not, said, "But there is never a thrush but can."

"What have thou taught Manes, thy serving-man?" Sylvius asked.

"To be as unlike thy sons as is possible," Diogenes said.

"He has taught me to fast, lie hard, and run away," Manes said.

"Lie hard" means 1) tell big lies, and 2) lie on the hard ground to sleep.

"What do thou say, Perim?" Sylvius asked. "Will thou be a student with Diogenes as your master?"

"Aye, as long as he will teach me first to run away," Perim said.

"Thou need not be taught because thy legs are so nimble," Diogenes said.

Perim was a dancer.

"What do thou say, Milo?" Sylvius asked. "Will thou be a student with Diogenes as your master?"

"Nay, hold your peace; he shall not," Diogenes said.

"Why?" Sylvius asked.

"There is not room enough for him and me to tumble both in one tub," Diogenes said.

Hmm. Indelicate, that.

"Well, Diogenes, I perceive that my sons cannot endure thy manners."

"I thought no less, when they knew my virtues," Diogenes said.

"Farewell, Diogenes, thou need not have to eat scraped roots, if thou would follow Alexander," Sylvius said.

"Nor would thou need to follow Alexander, if thou would eat scraped roots," Diogenes said.

Do as Alexander the Great wants you to do, and you will eat well.

Do as you want to do, and you will be free.

Alone, Apelles said to himself:

"I fear, Apelles, that thine eyes have blabbed that which thy tongue dared not reveal. What little regard for thy own safety had thou!

"While Alexander viewed the counterfeit [the picture] of Campaspe, thou stood gazing on her countenance [her face].

"If he spies your love for her, or only suspects it, thou must necessarily perish twice. Physically you will perish because of Alexander's hate, and metaphorically you will perish because of thine own love.

"Thy pale looks when he blushed with pleasure when seeing Campaspe's picture, thy sad countenance when he smiled, thy sighs when he asked questions, may breed in him a jealousy, and perhaps a frenzy.

"O love! I never before knew what thou were, and now thou have changed me so that I don't know what I myself am!

"Only this I know: that I must endure intolerable passions, for unknown — that is, inexperienced — pleasures.

"Don't dispute the cause, wretched Apelles, but yield to it: For it is better to melt with desire than to wrestle and contend with love. Cast thyself on thy filled-with-worries bed, be content to live unknown and inexperienced, and die unfound and undiscovered.

"O Campaspe, I have painted thee in my heart. Painted? Nay, contrary to my art of painting, I have imprinted thee in my heart; and I have imprinted thee in such deep characters that nothing can raze it out, unless it rubs my heart out."

Milectus, Phrygius, and Lais walked over to Diogenes, who was in his tub.

Lais was a courtesan, aka prostitute, and Milectus and Phrygius were soldiers in Alexander's army.

Milectus said, "It shall go hard, but this peace shall bring us some pleasure."

"It shall go hard" means "there will be trouble" if something doesn't happen as I want it to happen.

What he wanted to have happen was sexual pleasure.

"It" and "hard" had double meanings.

Phrygius said, "Down with arms, and up with legs: This is a world for the nonce — for this one purpose."

One meaning of "arms" is "weapons."

A prostitute's legs are frequently up.

Lais said:

"Sweet youths, if you knew what it was to save your sweet blood, you would not so foolishly go about to shed it in war.

"What delight can there be in gashing, to make foul scars in fair faces and crooked maims in straight legs?

"You youths do this as though men born well formed by nature would on purpose become deformed by folly; and all indeed for a newfound term, which is called 'valiant,' a word that breeds more quarrels than the sense — the word's meaning — can breed commendation."

"It is true, Lais, a featherbed has no equal, and good drink makes good blood," Milectus said. "And shall pelting, violent words spill it?"

"It" refers both to the drink and to the blood.

Phrygius said, "I mean to enjoy the world, and to draw out my life at the wiredrawer's, not to curtail it off at the cutler's."

A wiredrawer draws metal into wires.

Phrygius wanted a long life, not one cut short — curtailed — by a maker of knives and swords — a cutler.

Lais said:

"You may talk about war, speak big, conquer worlds with great words, but stay at home, where instead of alarms and calls to battles, you shall have dances, and instead of hot battles with fierce men, you shall have gentle skirmishes with fair women.

"These pewter coats of armor can never sit and fit as well as satin doublets. Believe me, you cannot conceive the pleasure of peace, unless you despise the rudeness and violence of war."

Milectus said:

"That is true.

"But look at Diogenes prying — looking at us — over his tub."

He called:

"Diogenes, what do thou say to such a morsel?"

He was referring to Lais, a morsel of female flesh.

"I say, I would spit it out of my mouth because it should not poison my stomach," Diogenes replied.

According to Laertius, "One of [Diogenes'] sayings was [...] that good-looking courtesans were like poisoned mead."

Mead is an alcohol-containing drink that is made with fermented honey and water.

"Thou speak as thou are: a rude Cynic," Phrygius said. "It is no meat for dogs."

"I am a dog, and philosophy berates me from carrion," Diogenes said.

His philosophy as a Cynic kept him away from rotting flesh (carrion) by berating him if he got near it.

Angry at being insulted, the anti-war prostitute Lais said to Diogenes, "Uncivil wretch, whose manners are answerable and conformable to thy calling as a Cynic, the time was that thou would have had my company, had it not been, as thou said, too dear."

"Dear" can mean "expensive."

"I remember there was a thing that I repented me of," Diogenes said, "and now thou have told it, it was indeed too dear of nothing, and thou dear to — beloved by — nobody."

"Too dear of nothing" means "even free is too high a price to pay for it" or "why pay anything for nothing?"

"Get down, villain," Lais said, as if she were speaking to a dog, "or I will have thy head broken."

"Will you crouch down?" Milectus asked Diogenes.

Phrygius said:

"Avant, cur! Get lost!"

Diogenes sank down in his tub.

Phrygius then said:

"Come, sweet Lais, let us go to some place and possess peace.

"But first let us sing. There is more pleasure in the tuning of a voice than there is in a volley of shot."

They sang.

Milectus said, "Now let us make haste to leave, lest Alexander finds us here."

They exited.

Alexander the Great and Hephestion talked together in the marketplace, near Diogenes' tub. A page was present.

Alexander the Great said, "I think, Hephestion, you are more melancholy now than you were accustomed to be, but I perceive it is all because of Alexander. You can neither brook and tolerate this peace, nor my pleasure, but now be of good cheer because although I close my eyes, I do not sleep."

Hephestion said, "I am not melancholy, nor am I well content, for I don't know how it happened, but there is such a rust crept into my bones with this long period of ease that I fear I shall not scour it out with infinite labors."

Alexander the Great said:

"Yes, yes, if all the travails and travels of conquering the world will set either thy body or mine in tune, we will undertake them.

"But what do you think about Apelles? Did you ever see anyone so perplexed? He neither answered directly to any question, nor looked steadfastly upon anything. I bet my life the painter is in love."

Hephestion said:

"It may be, for commonly we see that it is normal in artificers and artists to be enamored of their own works, as Archidamus was of his wooden dove, Pygmalion of his ivory image, and Arachne of his wooden swan.

"This is especially true of painters, who playing with their own imaginations, now desiring to draw a glancing eye, then a rolling eye, now a closing eye, still mending it, never ending it, until they are caught with it; and then — the poor souls! — they kiss the colors with their lips, with which before they were loath to taint their fingers."

Alexander the Great said:

"I will find out whether Apelles is in love.

"Page, go speedily for Apelles, tell him to come here, and when you see us earnestly in talk, suddenly cry out, 'Apelles' shop is on fire!'"

"It shall be done," the page said.

"Don't forget your lesson," Alexander the Great said. "Don't forget what I told you to say."

The page exited.

"I wonder what your trick shall be," Hephestion said.

"The event shall show that," Alexander the Great said.

"If he is in love, then I pity the poor painter," Hephestion said.

"Don't pity him, please; set aside that severe gravity and tell me what you think about love," Alexander the Great said.

"As the Macedonians do of their herb beet, which looking yellow in the ground, and black in the hand, think it better seen than touched," Hephestion said.

"But what do you imagine love is?" Alexander the Great asked.

"A word by superstition thought a god, by use turned to a humor, by self-will made a flattering madness," Hephestion said.

One meaning of "humor" is "mood."

The god of love is Cupid.

Alexander the Great said:

"You are too hard hearted to think so of love.

"Let us go to Diogenes."

After they had walked over to Diogenes' tub, Alexander the Great said:

"Diogenes, thou may think it somewhat of a big deal that Alexander comes to thee again so soon."

"If you have come to learn, you could not come soon enough," Diogenes said. "If you have come to laugh, you have come too soon."

"It would better become thee to be more courteous, and frame thyself to please others," Hephestion said.

"And it would better become you to be less courteous," Diogenes said. "You would be better if you would dare to displease."

"What do thou think of the time we have here?" Alexander the Great asked.

"That we have little, and lose much," Diogenes said.

"If someone is sick, what would thou have him do?" Alexander the Great asked.

"Be sure that he does not make his physician his heir," Diogenes said.

"If thou might have thy will, how much ground would content thee?" Alexander the Great asked.

"As much as you in the end must be contented with," Diogenes said.

"What! A world?" Alexander the Great asked.

"No, the length of my body," Diogenes said.

He meant a grave.

"Hephestion, shall I be a little pleasant and joke with him?" Alexander the Great asked.

"You may, but he will be very perverse with you," Hephestion said.

Alexander the Great said:

"It doesn't matter. I cannot be angry with him.

"Diogenes, I ask thee, what do thou think of love?"

"A little worser than I can of hate," Diogenes said.

"And why?" Alexander the Great asked.

"Because it is better to hate the things that cause one to love than to love the things that give occasion of hate," Diogenes said.

"Why, aren't women the best creatures in the world?" Alexander the Great asked.

"Next to men and bees," Diogenes said.

"What do thou dislike chiefly in a woman?" Alexander the Great asked.

"One thing," Diogenes said.

"What?" Alexander the Great asked.

"That she is a woman," Diogenes said.

Alexander the Great said:

"In my opinion thou were never born from a woman because thou think such hard opinions about women, but now comes Apelles, who I am sure is as far from thy thoughts as thou are from his cunning.

"Diogenes, I will have thy cabin moved nearer to my court because I will be a philosopher."

"And when you have done so, please move your court further from my cabin because I will not be a courtier," Diogenes said.

Apelles entered the scene.

Alexander the Great said:

"But here comes Apelles."

Diogenes disappeared into his tub.

Alexander the Great then asked:

"Apelles, what piece of work have you now in hand?"

"None in hand, if it pleases your majesty, but I am devising a platform — that is, I am planning a picture in my head," Apelles said.

"I think your hand put it in your head," Alexander the Great said. "Is it nothing about Venus?"

"No, but it is something above Venus," Apelles said.

The page shouted, "Apelles, Apelles, look around you — your shop is on fire!"

"Aye me!" Apelles said. "If the picture of Campaspe has been burnt, I am ruined!"

Alexander the Great said:

"Stay, Apelles, no haste: It is your heart that is on fire, not your shop; and if Campaspe does hang there, I wish she were burnt.

"But do you have the picture of Campaspe?

"It's likely that you love her well, since you don't care if all else is lost, as long as she is safe."

Making a king angry can be dangerous, so Apelles lied:

"I don't love her."

He continued:

"But your majesty knows that painters in their last — most recent — works are said to excel themselves, and in this I have so much pleased myself, that the shadow [painting] as much delights me as an artificer, as the substance does others who are amorous."

Alexander the Great replied:

"You lay your colors grossly — your pretense of not loving the real Campaspe is obvious. Although I could not paint in your shop, I can spy into your excuse.

"Don't be ashamed, Apelles, for it is a gentleman's sport to be in love."

Alexander ordered some attendants:

"Tell Campaspe to come here."

He then said to Apelles:

"I might have been made privy to your affection; although my counsel had not been necessary, yet my countenance — my permission — for you to love might have been thought requisite and necessary. But Apelles, in truth, thou did love secretly and under hand, yes, and under Alexander's nose, and — but I say no more."

Still wary, Apelles said, "Apelles does not love so, but he lives to do as Alexander wants him to."

Campaspe entered the scene.

"Campaspe, here is news," Alexander the Great said. "Apelles is in love with you."

"It pleases your majesty to say so," Campaspe said.

Alexander the Great whispered to Hephestion:

"Hephestion, I will test her, too."

He then said out loud:

"Campaspe, for the good qualities I know in Apelles, and the virtue I see in you, I am determined you shall enjoy one another.

"What do you say, Campaspe, would you say, 'Aye,' to marriage with Apelles?"

"Your handmaid must obey, if you command," Campaspe replied.

Like Apelles, Campaspe was wary of angering Alexander.

Alexander the Great whispered to Hephestion, "Don't you think, Hephestion, that she would like to be commanded?"

"I am no thought-catcher," Hephestion quietly replied, "but I guess unhappily and unfavorably when it comes to your love for her."

He could see that Campaspe wanted to marry Apelles, not be Alexander's concubine.

Alexander the Great said out loud to Campaspe, "I will not force marriage, where I cannot compel love."

He was teasing her by saying that he would not force her to marry Apelles.

Wanting to marry Apelles, Campaspe said, "But your majesty may raise the issue, where you are willing to have a match."

Alexander the Great said:

"Believe me, Hephestion, these parties are agreed; they would have me be both priest and witness.

"Apelles, take Campaspe."

Apelles hesitated.

Alexander the Great asked Apelles:

"Why don't you move over to her?"

He then said:

"Campaspe, take Apelles."

Campaspe hesitated.

Alexander the Great asked Campaspe:

"Won't this match be made?"

He then said to Apelles and Campaspe:

"If you are ashamed one of the other, you shall never come together by my consent."

He then said:

"But don't dissemble.

"Campaspe, do you love Apelles?"

"Pardon me, my lord," she said, "but I do love Apelles!"

Alexander the Great said:

"Apelles, it would be a shame for you, being loved so openly by so fair a virgin, to say the contrary.

"Do you love Campaspe?"

Apelles said, "I love only Campaspe!"

Alexander the Great said:

"These are two loving worms, Hephestion!

"I perceive that Alexander cannot subdue the passions and affections of men, although he conquers their countries.

"Love falls like a dew as well upon the low grass as upon the high cedar. Sparks have their heat, ants have their gall, flies have their spleen.

"Well, enjoy one another.

"I give her thee frankly, Apelles. Thou shall see that Alexander makes but a toy and trifle of love, and he leads affection and desire in fetters; and he chains fancy, using it as if it were a fool to make entertainment for him, or a minstrel to make him merry.

"It is not the amorous glance of an eye that can settle an idle thought in the heart.

"No, no, it is children's play: a life for seamsters and scholars. The seamsters pricking — sewing — in clothing have nothing else to think about, and the scholars picking fancies out of books have little else to marvel at.

"Go, Apelles, take with you your Campaspe.

"Alexander is cloyed and satiated with looking on that which thou marvel at."

According to Alexander the Great's words, he had grown tired of Campaspe.

Apelles knelt and said, "I give thanks to your majesty on bended knee. You have honored Apelles."

Campaspe curtsied and said, "I give thanks to you with my bowed heart. You have blessed Campaspe."

Apelles and Campaspe exited.

Alexander the Great said:

"Page, go warn Clitus and Parmenio and the other lords to be in a state of readiness.

"Let the trumpet sound, strike up the drum, and I will immediately go into Persia."

The page exited.

Alexander the Great then asked:

"How are things now, Hephestion? Is Alexander able to resist love as he chooses?"

"The conquering of Thebes was not as honorable as the subduing of these thoughts of love," Hephestion said.

Alexander the Great said:

"It would be a shame that Alexander should desire to command the world, if he could not command himself.

"But come, let us go. I will test whether I can better bear my hand with my heart than I could with my eye.

"And good Hephestion, when all the world is won, and every country is thine and mine, either find me out another country to subdue, or on my word I will fall in love."

— NOTES —
Diogenes

Recommended Good Reading:

Joshua J. Mark, "The Life of Diogenes of Sinope in Diogenes Laertius." *World History Encyclopedia*. 6 August 2014.

https://www.worldhistory.org/article/740/the-life-of-diogenes-of-sinope-in-diogenes-laertiu/

This is the Project Gutenberg translation; it is a free download:

Diogenes Laërtius, *The Lives and Opinions of Eminent Philosophers*. Translator: C. D. Yonge.

https://www.gutenberg.org/files/57342/57342-h/57342-h.htm

This link will take you to the chapter on Diogenes the Cynic:

https://www.gutenberg.org/files/57342/57342-h/57342-h.htm#Page_224

Plutarch. *Plutarch's Lives*. With an English Translation by Bernadotte Perrin. Cambridge, MA: Harvard University Press. London: William Heinemann Ltd., 1919.

http://www.perseus.tufts.edu/hopper/text?doc=Perseus%3Atext%3A1999.01.0243%3Achapter%3D1%3Asection%3I

Plutarch. *Life of Alexander*. Trans. John Dryden.

http://classics.mit.edu/Plutarch/alexandr.html

Campaspe and Apelles

Their story is told in Pliny, 35.36. Here is an excerpt:

It was a custom with Apelles, to which he most tenaciously adhered, never to let any day pass, however busy he might be, without exercising himself by tracing some outline or other; a practice which has now passed into a proverb. It was also a practice with him, when he had completed a work, to exhibit it to the view of the passers-by in some exposed place; while he himself, concealed behind the picture, would listen to the criticisms that were passed upon it; it being his opinion that the judgment of the public was preferable to his own, as being the more discerning of the two. It was under these circumstances, they say, that he was censured by a shoemaker for having represented the shoes with one shoe-string too little. The next day, the shoemaker, quite proud at seeing the former error corrected, thanks to his advice, began to criticize the leg; upon which Apelles, full of indignation, popped his head out, and reminded him that a shoemaker should give no opinion beyond the shoes, a piece of advice which has equally passed into a proverbial saying. In fact, Apelles was a person of great amenity of manners, a circumstance which rendered him particularly agreeable to Alexander the Great, who would often come to his studio. He had forbidden himself, by public edict, as already stated, to be represented by any other artist. On one occasion, however, when the prince was in his studio, talking a great deal about painting without knowing anything about it, Apelles quietly begged that he would quit the subject, telling him that he would get laughed at by the boys who were there grinding the colours: so great was the influence which he rightfully possessed over a monarch, who was otherwise of an irascible temperament. And yet, irascible as he was, Alexander conferred upon him a very signal mark of the high estimation in which he held him; for having, in his admiration of her extraordinary beauty, engaged Apelles to paint Pancaste [Campaspe] undraped,50[1] the most beloved of all his concubines, the artist while so engaged, fell in love with her; upon which, Alexander, perceiving this to be the case, made him a present of her, thus showing himself, though a great king in courage, a still greater one in self-command, this action redounding no less to his honour than any of his victories. For in thus conquering himself, not only did he sacrifice his passions in favor of the artist, but even his affections as well; uninfluenced, too, by the feelings which must have possessed his favorite in thus passing at once from the arms of a monarch to those of a painter. Some persons are of opinion that Pancaste was the model of Apelles in his painting of Venus Anadyomene.

50: Also known as "Campaspe," and "Pacate." She was the favorite concubine of Alexander, and is said to have been his first love.

Source of Above: Bostock, John, and Riley, H.T., transl. Pliny the Elder. *The Natural History*. London: Henry G. Bohn, 1855. Accessed 16 October 2022. https://www.perseus.tufts.edu/hopper/ text?doc=Perseus%3Atext%3A1999.02.0137%3Abook%3D35%3Achapter%3D

---

1. https://www.perseus.tufts.edu/hopper/

text?doc=Perseus%3Atext%3A1999.02.0137%3Abook%3D35%3Achapter%3D36#note50

— 1.1 —

Timoclea

In the play, Timoclea is treated well. But in history, she was treated badly (and then acted courageously) before Alexander saw her.

This is from Plutarch's "Life of Alexander":

Among the other calamities that befell the city, it happened that some Thracian soldiers, having broken into the house of a matron of high character and repute, named Timoclea, their captain, after he had used violence with her, to satisfy his avarice as well as lust, asked her, if she knew of any money concealed; to which she readily answered she did, and bade him follow her into a garden, where she showed him a well, into which, she told him, upon the taking of the city, she had thrown what she had of most value. The greedy Thracian presently stooping down to view the place where he thought the treasure lay, she came behind him and pushed him into the well, and then flung great stones in upon him, till she had killed him. After which, when the soldiers led her away bound to Alexander, her very mien and gait showed her to be a woman of dignity, and of a mind no less elevated, not betraying the least sign of fear or astonishment. And when the king asked her who she was, "I am," said she, "the sister of Theagenes, who fought the battle of Chaeronea with your father Philip, and fell there in command for the liberty of Greece." Alexander was so surprised, both at what she had done and what she said, that he could not choose but give her and her children their freedom to go whither they pleased.

Source: Plutarch. *Life of Alexander.* Trans. John Dryden. Accessed 16 October 2022.

http://classics.mit.edu/Plutarch/alexandr.html

— 1.3 —

The source of the quotation from Laertius is this book:

Diogenes Laertius, *Lives of Eminent Philosophers*. R.D. Hicks, Trans. The Loeb Classical Library. London: William Heineman. New York: G.P. Putnam's Sons, 1925. P. 25.

— 1.3 —

Source of Zhang Liang Story: Wang Xuanming, *Three Strategies of Huang Shi Gong*. Singapore: Asiapac Books PTE LTD, 1993, pp. 2-8. Retold by David Bruce.

— 1.3 —

In 1.3, the philosophers discuss the existence of God, mentioning the Prime Mover.

For Your Information:

St. Thomas Aquinas (1225-1274): The Five Ways

One of the greatest geniuses of all time is Saint Thomas Aquinas (1225-1274), author of the Summa Theologica, which gave the Catholic Church much of its philosophy and theology. Certainly Aquinas is recognized for his valuable contributions to the Catholic Church, as he was canonized in 1323.

Aquinas believed in a twofold approach to knowledge of God. First, he believed in revelation: The Bible provides us with knowledge of God. Second, Aquinas engages in natural theology: Through our reason and our knowledge of Nature, we can arrive at knowledge of God. For example, Aquinas believed that there are five ways to prove the existence of God. Each of these five ways is based upon a fact found in Nature.

Aquinas assumes a principle of reason that we call the Principle of Sufficient Reason. According to the Principle of Sufficient Reason, there is an explanation or cause for everything. According to the Principle of Sufficient Reason, when something exists, we can ask for a reason sufficient to explain the existence of that thing.

The Five Ways

I. The Argument From Change

Take a look at Nature. What do you see? One of the things that you will see is that things change. The seasons change, an infant grows up into an old person, day succeeds night, and night succeeds day — change is constant. Therefore we can ask, "Why is there change? What is a reason to explain the existence of change?" According to the Principle of Sufficient Reason, there is a reason sufficient to explain the fact of change.

Aquinas comes up with two possible answers:

1. We may refer to an infinite series of changes. This thing changed because that thing changed, and that thing changed because this other thing changed, etc. Saint Thomas rejects this answer because "then there would be no first mover, and, consequently, no other mover, seeing that subsequent movers move only inasmuch as they are moved by the first mover ... ."

2. An Unmoved Mover, or Prime Mover, exists. The Unmoved Mover is itself unchanging, but it is the source from which all particular instances of change proceed. Since there are only two possibilities, and Aquinas has rejected the first possibility, the second possibility must be true.

In Aquinas' words, "Therefore it is necessary to arrive at a first mover, moved by no other; and this everyone understands to be God."

II. The Argument From Causality

The Argument From Causality works the same way as the Argument From Change. Take a look at Nature. What do you see? One of the things you will see is that things are caused. One thing causes another, and that causes another. The frost causes leaves to die and turn colors, and that in turn causes the leaves to fall off the tree. The weather in part causes the leaves to decompose and to return to the soil, from whence it fertilizes plants. Causation is all around us. Therefore we can ask, "Why does causation exist?" According to the Principle of Sufficient Reason, there is a reason sufficient to explain the fact of causation.

Once again, there are two possibilities:

1. We may refer to an infinite series of causes. This thing was caused by that thing, and that thing in turn was caused by this other thing, etc. Saint Thomas rejects this answer because he believes that there must be a first cause that starts the series of causes. Without the first cause, there would be no effect that would be the second cause.

2. A First Cause, which is itself uncaused, exists. The First Cause is itself uncaused, but it is the source from which all particular instances of causation proceed. Since there are only two possibilities, and Aquinas has rejected the first possibility, the second possibility must be true.

In Aquinas' words, "Therefore it is necessary to admit a first ... cause, which everyone gives the name of God."

III. The Argument From Possibility and Necessity

The Argument From Possibility and Necessity follows the same pattern as Aquinas' first two arguments. Look around at Nature: What do you see? Everywhere you see contingent being. Definition: A contingent being is a merely possible being; there is no necessity for it to exist. My existence is contingent. I am here because my parents exist. My parents in turn exist because of their parents. A desk is an example of contingent being. The desk did not have to exist — it exists only because someone decided to make it. Contingency exists throughout Nature. Therefore, we can ask, "Why does contingency exist?" According to the Principle of Sufficient Reason, there is a reason sufficient to explain the fact of contingency.

Once again, there are two possibilities:

1. We may refer to an infinite series of instances of contingency. This thing is contingent upon that thing, and that thing in turn is contingent upon this other thing, etc. Saint Thomas rejects this answer because if everything is contingent, then at one time nothing existed. If that had happened, then nothing would exist today. But of course something exists today, so it is not true that everything is contingent.

2. A Necessary Being, or Prime Mover, which is itself not contingent upon anything, exists. The Necessary Being is itself not contingent, but it is the source from which all particular instances of contingency proceed. Since there are only two possibilities, and Aquinas has rejected the first possibility, the second possibility must be true.

In Aquinas' words, "Therefore we cannot but admit the existence of some being having of itself its necessity, and not receiving it from another, but rather causing in others their necessity. This all men speak of as God."

IV. The Argument From Gradations of Nature

Once again, we have an argument with the same structure as the first three arguments. Look at Nature. What do you see? You see varying degrees of excellence. This being is better than that being. This being is truer than that being. This being is nobler than that being. On every hand, we see varying degrees of excellence. Therefore, we can ask, "Why are there degrees of excellence?" According to the Principle of Sufficient Reason, there is a reason sufficient to explain the fact of varying degrees of excellence.

Once again, there are two possibilities:

1. We may refer to an infinite series of degrees of excellence. This being is better than that being, and that being in turn is better than this other being, and so on to infinity. Saint Thomas rejects this answer because there must be a standard — a "maximum" — according to which we judge things.

2. Perfect Being exists. Perfect Being has all manner of perfections, and through our knowledge of Perfect Being, we are able to recognize imperfect being, or varying degrees of excellence, in Nature. Since there are only two possibilities, and Aquinas has rejected the first possibility, the second possibility must be true.

In Aquinas' words, "Therefore there must also be something which is to all beings the cause of their being, goodness, and every other perfection; and this we call God."

V. The Argument From Design

The fifth way of proving that God exists is a little different from the first four arguments. Look at Nature. What do you see? Everywhere you see design. For example, we need eyes to see, and we have eyes. Everything in Nature — including natural bodies that lack knowledge — seems to have an end; everywhere we see design. Therefore, we can ask, "Why is there design in Nature?" According to the Principle of Sufficient Reason, there is a reason sufficient to explain design.

Once again, there are two possibilities:

1. All the design we see in Nature occurred by chance. In an infinite amount of time, the universe arrived at the stage of development we see today. Saint Thomas rejects this answer because Nature appears to be working toward an end — the end being the development of intelligent life that can become children of God. And nothing can work toward an end "unless it be directed by some being endowed with knowledge and intelligence."

2. There must be a Designer of Nature, and this Designer uses intelligence to achieve His aims. Since there are only two possibilities, and Aquinas has rejected the first possibility, the second possibility must be true.

In Aquinas' words, "Therefore some intelligent being exists by whom all natural things are directed to their end; and this being we call God."

Conclusion

Put all the proofs together, and we know that God is unchanging (the First Way), uncaused (the Second Way), necessary (the Third Way), perfect (the Fourth Way), and providential (the Fifth Way).

Note: *The quotations by Aquinas that appear in this essay are from his Summa Theologica, Question 2, Article 3, in Introduction to Saint Thomas Aquinas, edited by Anton C. Pegis.*

Source: David Bruce. *Philosophy for the Masses: Religion.*
https://www.smashwords.com/books/view/376026
https://drive.google.com/file/d/
10Pkuj2HT64Ug5oq6dy3fc5oqnnVAFi7I/view?usp=sharing
For Your Information:

C. S. Lewis (1898-1963): The Argument From Morality

C. S. Lewis wrote about the Moral Argument in his book Mere Christianity (1952). Of course, Lewis is famous for many things, not just for being a defender of the faith in many of his books. For example, he wrote the wonderful children's series The Chronicles of Narnia, which I have read several times. In addition, Shadowlands is a nonfiction movie about Lewis' marriage to the American poet Joy Davidman.

The Moral Argument argues that God is the best explanation for Humankind's experience of a Moral Law within themselves. As such, it uses the Principle of Sufficient Reason. We find an objective moral law within ourselves; what is a reason sufficient to explain the existence of this moral law?

It is an important presupposition of the Moral Argument that the Moral Law is objective and not subjective. If the Moral Law is subjective, then ethics is a matter of opinion. What I believe is right, is right for me, and what you believe is right, is right for you. The same applies to what each of us believes to be wrong.

One consequence of subjectivism is that the same thing can be both right and wrong at the same time. Thus, I may think that rape is morally right and you may think that rape is morally wrong, and if subjectivism is the correct ethical theory, then both of us are correct in what we believe. Thus, rape is morally right for me but morally wrong for you.

Objectivism, however, denies this. According to objectivism, moral rules exist that apply to everyone, no matter what we may believe about them. Thus, according to objectivism, the truth of the statement "Rape is wrong" is not a matter of opinion. The statement is either true or false. If the statement is true, then this moral rule applies to everyone, at every time, in every place, no matter what they may believe about the statement.

Note that although objectivism requires that ethical statements (e.g. "Rape is wrong" and "Murder is wrong") be either true or false — they are not a matter of opinion — objectivism does not require the belief that every human being have an innate moral sense that tells them what to do. (We may have to be educated about what is morally right and what is morally wrong; after all, we have to be taught calculus, which is definitely objective.) In addition, objectivism does not require that all persons naturally and easily know what is morally right and what is morally wrong. Objectivism merely requires that ethical statements be true or false. We may not know whether a certain ethical statement is true or false — objectivism merely requires that it be true or false.

As you know, Lewis will argue that God is the best explanation of the Moral Law. However, many people would like to argue that human beings are the source of the Moral Law. Of course, if this were true, then the Moral Law would be subjective and not objective. An argument for human beings as the source of the Moral Law could state that certain moral laws came into effect because they were useful in helping communities to exist. However, a subjectivist who argues this could not argue that it is objectively better for communities to exist than not to *exist. Lewis believes in an objective moral law that he calls the Law of [Human] Nature or the Law of Decent Behavior.*

Lewis starts his argument from human experience: There are two odd things we notice about members of the human species:

1) They have an idea about the kind of behavior they ought to practice.

2) They do not, in fact, always practice this kind of behavior.

Because of these two things, the human species is much different from a stone or a tree. After all, a stone or a tree does not think about what it ought to do; in addition, a stone or a tree always does what it is supposed to do. If you drop a stone, the stone does not suddenly take thought and remember that now it is supposed to fall to the ground. Instead, it is a nonthinking thing and obeys unquestioningly the law of gravity.

We know that there is a Moral Law that human beings are aware of, but that stones and trees are not aware of. The next question is, What is a reason sufficient to explain the existence of the Moral Law?

Lewis writes that there are two main views of the existence of the universe:

1) The Materialist view: According to this view, the universe just happened to exist.

2) The Religious view: According to this view, "what is behind the universe is more like a mind than it is like anything else we know. That is, it is conscious, and has purposes, and prefers one thing to another. And on this view it made the universe, partly for purposes we do not know, but partly, at any rate, in order to produce creatures like itself — I mean, like itself to the extent of having minds."

In trying to decide which view is correct, we cannot have recourse to science, because science cannot answer such questions as these: Why is there a universe? and Why does it go on as it does? and Has it any meaning?

The only way that we can answer this question is from our observation of ourselves. Within ourselves, we find a Moral Law — a Moral Law that the physical universe is unable to account for. The best explanation of the Moral Law is that a mind is behind the universe, making the universe what it is.

The Materialist view of the universe cannot explain the existence of the Moral Law because, as Lewis states, you can hardly imagine a bit of matter telling you what is right and what is wrong. (According to Materialism, all reality consists of matter and the manifestations of matter. Materialism has no room for a nonmaterial mind or spirit.)

The only other view of the universe is the Religious view, which states that there is a Mind behind the universe Who directs the universe. Lewis writes, "The only way in which we could expect [the Mind] to show itself would be inside ourselves as an influence or a command trying to get us to behave in a certain way." Of course, this is an exact description of the Moral Law we find within ourselves. Lewis' conclusion at this point is this:

"I am not yet within a hundred miles of the God of Christian theology. All I have got at this point is a Something which is directing the universe, and which appears in me as a law urging me to do right and making me feel responsible and uncomfortable when I do wrong. I think we have to assume it is more like a mind than it is like anything else we know — because after all the only other thing we know is matter and you can hardly imagine a bit of matter giving instructions."

Lewis uses logical reasoning in his essay. He writes that there are two candidates for explaining the existence of the Moral Law: Materialism and Religion. Since Materialism cannot explain why the Moral Law exists, then the Religious answer must be the correct one.

In a short note, Lewis mentions an alternative to the Materialist view and the Religious view: the Life-Force Philosophy (aka Creative Evolution and Emergent Evolution). According to this view, "the small variations by which life on this planet 'evolved' from the lowest forms to Man were not due to chance but to the 'striving' or 'purposiveness' of a Life-Force." Lewis asks people who hold this view "whether by Life-Force they mean something with a mind or not." If they do, then they really hold the Religious view. If they don't, then they are talking nonsense, for what sense does it make to say that "something without a mind 'strives' or has 'purposes'?"

Lewis completely rejects the Life-Force Philosophy. He writes, "The Life-Force is a sort of tame God. You can switch it on when you want, but it will not bother you. All the thrills of religion and none of the cost. Is the Life-Force the greatest achievement of wishful thinking the world has yet seen?"

Note*: The quotations by C. S. Lewis that appear in this essay are from his Mere Christianity (London: Geoffrey Bles, 1952).*

Source: David Bruce. *Philosophy for the Masses: Religion.*
https://www.smashwords.com/books/view/376026
https://drive.google.com/file/d/
10Pkuj2HT64Ug5oq6dy3fc5oqnnVAFi7I/view?usp=sharing

— 2.2 —

For Your Information:

But since that philosopher took not the slightest notice of Alexander, and continued to enjoy his leisure in the suburb Craneion, Alexander went in person to see him; and he found him lying in the sun. Diogenes raised himself up a little when he saw so many persons coming towards him, and fixed his eyes upon Alexander. And when that monarch addressed him with greetings, and asked if he wanted anything, 'Yes,' said Diogenes, 'stand a little out of my sun.' It is said that Alexander was so struck by this, and admired so much the haughtiness and grandeur of the man who had nothing but scorn for him, that he said to his followers, who were laughing and jesting about the philosopher as they went away, 'But verily, if I were not Alexander, I would be Diogenes.'

Plutarch. *Plutarch's Lives*. With an English Translation by Bernadotte Perrin. Cambridge, MA: Harvard University Press. London: William Heinemann Ltd., 1919.

http://www.perseus.tufts.edu/hopper/text?doc=Perseus:abo:tlg,0007,047:14

— 3.1 —

Ganymede as Catamite: Martial, Epigram 2

In the sixth line of Epigram 2 (page 34) a pun seems to be intended on the word pocula, which is used in the double meaning of a drinking cup and the anus. Therefore, 'mingles luscious cups' also means allows sodomy to be committed upon him. Martial writes:

Dulcia Dardanio nondum miscente ministro

Pocula, Juno fuit pro Ganymede Jovi.

[Translation]

Before the Dardanian servitor mingled Jove's sweet cups,

Juno was to him as Ganymede (i.e. acted as his catamite).

Source: "Sodomy with Women."
https://www.sacred-texts.com/cla/priap/prp101.htm

— 3.1 —

The story of Odysseus and Penelope's bed comes from my retelling of Homer's *Odyssey*:

Source: Bruce, David. *Homer's Odyssey: A Retelling in Prose.*
https://www.smashwords.com/books/view/87553
https://drive.google.com/file/d/
1rn5b3A6TFJngdZ_DC0daL9jZBToiSy-P/view?usp=sharing

For Your Information:

This famous letter was unquestionably not sent. The positive evidence is that the original remained with Franklin's papers. The negative evidence is that Strahan later gave no sign that he had received such a blast: when he responded on September 6 to a letter, now lost, from Franklin two days after this one, and when he wrote again on October 4, he showed the pain and sorrow that one friend reserves for the other's delusions, and also the implicit assumption that the relationship remained intact. On the rare occasions when Franklin lost his temper he was likely to recover it quickly. This outburst was an example in point: it relieved his rage at what was happening, and went no further.

Philada. July 5. 1775

Mr. Strahan,

You are a Member of Parliament, and one of that Majority which has doomed my Country to Destruction. You have begun to burn our Towns, and murder our People. Look upon your Hands! They are stained with the Blood of your Relations! You and I were long Friends: You are now my Enemy, and I am, Yours,

B Franklin

Source: "From Benjamin Franklin to William Strahan, 5 July 1775." Founders Online. National Archive. Accessed 20 October 2022. https://founders.archives.gov/documents/Franklin/01-22-02-0052

APPENDIX A: FAIR USE

§ 107. Limitations on exclusive rights: Fair use

Release date: 2004-04-30

Notwithstanding the provisions of sections 106 and 106A, the fair use of a copyrighted work, including such use by reproduction in copies or phonorecords or by any other means specified by that section, for purposes such as criticism, comment, news reporting, teaching (including multiple copies for classroom use), scholarship, or research, is not an infringement of copyright. In determining whether the use made of a work in any particular case is a fair use the factors to be considered shall include —

(1) the purpose and character of the use, including whether such use is of a commercial nature or is for nonprofit educational purposes;

(2) the nature of the copyrighted work;

(3) the amount and substantiality of the portion used in relation to the copyrighted work as a whole; and

(4) the effect of the use upon the potential market for or value of the copyrighted work.

The fact that a work is unpublished shall not itself bar a finding of fair use if such finding is made upon consideration of all the above factors.

Source of Fair Use information:

http://www.law.cornell.edu/uscode/17/107.html

APPENDIX B: ABOUT THE AUTHOR

It was a dark and stormy night. Suddenly a cry rang out, and on a hot summer night in 1954, Josephine, wife of Carl Bruce, gave birth to a boy — me. Unfortunately, this young married couple allowed Reuben Saturday, Josephine's brother, to name their first-born. Reuben, aka "The Joker," decided that Bruce was a nice name, so he decided to name me Bruce Bruce. I have gone by my middle name — David — ever since.

Being named Bruce David Bruce hasn't been all bad. Bank tellers remember me very quickly, so I don't often have to show an ID. It can be fun in charades, also. When I was a counselor as a teenager at Camp Echoing Hills in Warsaw, Ohio, a fellow counselor gave the signs for "sounds like" and "two words," then she pointed to a bruise on her leg twice. Bruise Bruise? Oh yeah, Bruce Bruce is the answer!

Uncle Reuben, by the way, gave me a haircut when I was in kindergarten. He cut my hair short and shaved a small bald spot on the back of my head. My mother wouldn't let me go to school until the bald spot grew out again.

Of all my brothers and sisters (six in all), I am the only transplant to Athens, Ohio. I was born in Newark, Ohio, and have lived all around Southeastern Ohio. However, I moved to Athens to go to Ohio University and have never left.

At Ohio U, I never could make up my mind whether to major in English or Philosophy, so I got a bachelor's degree with a double major in both areas, then I added a Master of Arts degree in English and a Master of Arts degree in Philosophy. Yes, I have my MAMA degree.

Currently, and for a long time to come (I eat fruits and veggies), I am spending my retirement writing books such as *Nadia Comaneci: Perfect 10*, *The Funniest People in Comedy*, *Homer's* Iliad: *A Retelling in Prose*, and *William Shakespeare's* Hamlet: *A Retelling in Prose*.

If all goes well, I will publish one or two books a year for the rest of my life. (On the other hand, a good way to make God laugh is to tell Her your plans.)

By the way, my sister Brenda Kennedy writes romances such as *A New Beginning* and *Shattered Dreams*.

APPENDIX C: SOME BOOKS BY DAVID BRUCE

Retellings of a Classic Work of Literature

Arden of Faversham: *A Retelling*

Ben Jonson's The Alchemist: *A Retelling*

Ben Jonson's The Arraignment, or Poetaster: *A Retelling*

Ben Jonson's Bartholomew Fair: *A Retelling*

Ben Jonson's The Case is Altered: *A Retelling*

Ben Jonson's Catiline's Conspiracy: *A Retelling*

Ben Jonson's The Devil is an Ass: *A Retelling*

Ben Jonson's Epicene: *A Retelling*

Ben Jonson's Every Man in His Humor: *A Retelling*

Ben Jonson's Every Man Out of His Humor: *A Retelling*

Ben Jonson's The Fountain of Self-Love, or Cynthia's Revels: *A Retelling*

Ben Jonson's The Magnetic Lady, or Humors Reconciled: *A Retelling*

Ben Jonson's The New Inn, or The Light Heart: *A Retelling*

Ben Jonson's Sejanus' Fall: *A Retelling*

Ben Jonson's The Staple of News: *A Retelling*

Ben Jonson's A Tale of a Tub: *A Retelling*

Ben Jonson's Volpone, or the Fox: *A Retelling*

Christopher Marlowe's Complete Plays: Retellings

Christopher Marlowe's Dido, Queen of Carthage: *A Retelling*

Christopher Marlowe's Doctor Faustus: *Retellings of the 1604 A-Text and of the 1616 B-Text*

Christopher Marlowe's Edward II: *A Retelling*

Christopher Marlowe's The Massacre at Paris: *A Retelling*

Christopher Marlowe's The Rich Jew of Malta: *A Retelling*

Christopher Marlowe's Tamburlaine, Parts 1 and 2: *Retellings*

Dante's Divine Comedy: *A Retelling in Prose*

Dante's Inferno: *A Retelling in Prose*

Dante's Purgatory: *A Retelling in Prose*

Dante's Paradise: *A Retelling in Prose*

The Famous Victories of Henry V: *A Retelling*

From the Iliad *to the* Odyssey: *A Retelling in Prose of Quintus of Smyrna's* Posthomerica

George Chapman, Ben Jonson, and John Marston's Eastward Ho! *A Retelling*

George Peele's The Arraignment of Paris: *A Retelling*

George Peele's The Battle of Alcazar: *A Retelling*

George's Peele's David and Bathsheba, and the Tragedy of Absalom: *A Retelling*

George Peele's Edward I: *A Retelling*

George Peele's The Old Wives' Tale: *A Retelling*

George-a-Greene: *A Retelling*

The History of King Leir: *A Retelling*

Homer's Iliad: *A Retelling in Prose*

Homer's Odyssey: *A Retelling in Prose*

J.W. Gent.'s The Valiant Scot: *A Retelling*

Jason and the Argonauts: A Retelling in Prose of Apollonius of Rhodes' Argonautica

John Ford: Eight Plays Translated into Modern English

John Ford's The Broken Heart: *A Retelling*

John Ford's The Fancies, Chaste and Noble: *A Retelling*

John Ford's The Lady's Trial: *A Retelling*

John Ford's The Lover's Melancholy: *A Retelling*

John Ford's Love's Sacrifice: *A Retelling*

John Ford's Perkin Warbeck: *A Retelling*

John Ford's The Queen: *A Retelling*

John Ford's 'Tis Pity She's a Whore: *A Retelling*

John Lyly's Campaspe: *A Retelling*

John Lyly's Endymion, The Man in the Moon: *A Retelling*

John Lyly's Galatea: *A Retelling*

John Lyly's Love's Metamorphosis: *A Retelling*

John Lyly's Midas: *A Retelling*

John Lyly's Mother Bombie: *A Retelling*

John Lyly's Sappho and Phao: *A Retelling*

John Lyly's The Woman in the Moon: *A Retelling*

John Webster's The White Devil: *A Retelling*

King Edward III: *A Retelling*

Mankind: *A Medieval Morality Play* (A Retelling)

Margaret Cavendish's The Unnatural Tragedy: *A Retelling*

The Merry Devil of Edmonton: *A Retelling*

The Summoning of Everyman: *A Medieval Morality Play* (A Retelling)

Robert Greene's Friar Bacon and Friar Bungay: *A Retelling*

The Taming of a Shrew: *A Retelling*

Tarlton's Jests: A Retelling

Thomas Middleton's A Chaste Maid in Cheapside: *A Retelling*

Thomas Middleton's Women Beware Women: *A Retelling*

Thomas Middleton and Thomas Dekker's The Roaring Girl: *A Retelling*

Thomas Middleton and William Rowley's The Changeling: *A Retelling*

The Trojan War and Its Aftermath: Four Ancient Epic Poems

Virgil's Aeneid: *A Retelling in Prose*

William Shakespeare's 5 Late Romances: Retellings in Prose

William Shakespeare's 10 Histories: Retellings in Prose

William Shakespeare's 11 Tragedies: Retellings in Prose

William Shakespeare's 12 Comedies: Retellings in Prose

William Shakespeare's 38 Plays: Retellings in Prose
William Shakespeare's 1 Henry IV, aka Henry IV, Part 1: *A Retelling in Prose*
William Shakespeare's 2 Henry IV, aka Henry IV, Part 2: *A Retelling in Prose*
William Shakespeare's 1 Henry VI, aka Henry VI, Part 1: *A Retelling in Prose*
William Shakespeare's 2 Henry VI, aka Henry VI, Part 2: *A Retelling in Prose*
William Shakespeare's 3 Henry VI, aka Henry VI, Part 3: *A Retelling in Prose*
William Shakespeare's All's Well that Ends Well: *A Retelling in Prose*
William Shakespeare's Antony and Cleopatra: *A Retelling in Prose*
William Shakespeare's As You Like It: *A Retelling in Prose*
William Shakespeare's The Comedy of Errors: *A Retelling in Prose*
William Shakespeare's Coriolanus: *A Retelling in Prose*
William Shakespeare's Cymbeline: *A Retelling in Prose*
William Shakespeare's Hamlet: *A Retelling in Prose*
William Shakespeare's Henry V: *A Retelling in Prose*
William Shakespeare's Henry VIII: *A Retelling in Prose*
William Shakespeare's Julius Caesar: *A Retelling in Prose*
William Shakespeare's King John: *A Retelling in Prose*
William Shakespeare's King Lear: *A Retelling in Prose*
William Shakespeare's Love's Labor's Lost: *A Retelling in Prose*
William Shakespeare's Macbeth: *A Retelling in Prose*
William Shakespeare's Measure for Measure: *A Retelling in Prose*
William Shakespeare's The Merchant of Venice: *A Retelling in Prose*
William Shakespeare's The Merry Wives of Windsor: *A Retelling in Prose*
William Shakespeare's A Midsummer Night's Dream: *A Retelling in Prose*
William Shakespeare's Much Ado About Nothing: *A Retelling in Prose*
William Shakespeare's Othello: *A Retelling in Prose*
William Shakespeare's Pericles, Prince of Tyre: *A Retelling in Prose*
William Shakespeare's Richard II: *A Retelling in Prose*
William Shakespeare's Richard III: *A Retelling in Prose*
William Shakespeare's Romeo and Juliet: *A Retelling in Prose*
William Shakespeare's The Taming of the Shrew: *A Retelling in Prose*
William Shakespeare's The Tempest: *A Retelling in Prose*
William Shakespeare's Timon of Athens: *A Retelling in Prose*
William Shakespeare's Titus Andronicus: *A Retelling in Prose*
William Shakespeare's Troilus and Cressida: *A Retelling in Prose*
William Shakespeare's Twelfth Night: *A Retelling in Prose*
William Shakespeare's The Two Gentlemen of Verona: *A Retelling in Prose*
William Shakespeare's The Two Noble Kinsmen: *A Retelling in Prose*
William Shakespeare's The Winter's Tale: *A Retelling in Prose*